Frederick C. Hipkins

Repton and its Neighbourhood

a descriptive guide of the archæology, &c. of the district

Frederick C. Hipkins

Repton and its Neighbourhood
a descriptive guide of the archæology, &c. of the district

ISBN/EAN: 9783337368487

Printed in Europe, USA, Canada, Australia, Japan

Cover: Foto ©Andreas Hilbeck / pixelio.de

More available books at **www.hansebooks.com**

REPTON

AND ITS NEIGHBOURHOOD:

A DESCRIPTIVE GUIDE OF
THE ARCHÆOLOGY, &c., OF THE DISTRICT.

Illustrated by Photogravures, &c.

BY

F. C. HIPKINS, M.A., F.S.A.,

ASSISTANT MASTER AT REPTON SCHOOL.

SECOND EDITION.

A. J. LAWRENCE, PRINTER, REPTON
MDCCCXCIX.

PREFACE.

IN the year 1892, I ventured to write, for Reptonians, a short History of Repton, its quick sale emboldened me to set about obtaining materials for a second edition. The list of Authors, &c., consulted (printed at the end of this preface), will enable any one, who wishes to do so, to investigate the various events further, or to prove the truth of the facts recorded. Round the Church, Priory, and School centre all that is interesting, and, naturally, they occupy nearly all the pages of this second attempt to supply all the information possible to those who live in, or visit our old world village, whose church, &c., might well have served the poet Gray as the subject of his Elegy.

> "Beneath those rugged Elms, that Yew-tree's shade,
> Where heaves the Turf in many a mould'ring Heap,
> Each in his narrow Cell for ever laid,
> The rude Forefathers of the Hamlet sleep."

In writing the history of Repton certain events stand out more prominently than others, *e g*, the Conversion of Mercia by Diuma, its first bishop, and his assistant missionaries, Adda, Betti, and Cedda, the brother of St. Chad : the Founding of the Monastery during the reign

a

of Peada or his brother Wulphere (A.D. 655—675): the
coming of the Danes in 874, and the destruction of the
Abbey and town by them: the first building of Repton
Church, probably during the reign of Edgar the Peaceable, A.D. 957: the Founding of the Priory by Maud,
Countess of Chester, about the year 1150, its dissolution
in 1538, its destruction in 1553, and the Founding of the
School in 1557. Interwoven with these events are others
which have been recorded in the Chronicles, Histories,
Registers, &c., consulted, quoted, and used to produce
as interesting an account as possible of those events,
which extend over a period of nearly twelve hundred and
fifty years!

The hand of time, and man, especially the latter,
has gradually destroyed anything ancient, and "restorations" have completely changed the aspect of the village.
The Church, Priory, Hall, and "Cross," still serve as
links between the centuries, but, excepting these, only
one old house remains, in Well Lane, bearing initials
"T.S." and date "1686."

Even the Village Cross was restored! Down to the
year 1806, the shaft was square, with square capital, in
which an iron cross was fixed. In Bigsby's History of
Repton, (p. 261), there is a drawing of it, and an account
of its restoration, by the Rev. R. R. Rawlins.

During the last fifteen years the old house which
stood at the corner, (adjoining Mr Cattley's house,)
in which the "*Court Leet*" was held, and the "round-
house" at the back of the Post Office, with its octagonal-

shaped walls and roof, and oak door, studded with iron nails, have also been destroyed.

The consequence is that the History of Repton is chiefly concerned with ancient and mediæval times.

The Chapters on the Neighbourhood of Repton have been added in the hope that they may prove useful to those who may wish to make expeditions to the towns and villages mentioned. More might have been included, and more written about them, the great difficulty was to curtail both, and at the same time make an interesting, and intelligible record of the chief points of interest in the places described.

In conclusion, I wish to return thanks to those who by their advice, and information have helped me, especially the Rev. J. Charles Cox, LL.D., Author of "Derbyshire Churches," &c., J. T. Irvine, Esq., and Messrs. John Thompson and Sons who most kindly supplied me with plans of Crypt, and Church, made during the restorations of 1885- 6.

For the many beautiful photographs, my best thanks are due to Miss M. H. Barham, W. B. Hawkins, Esq., and C. B. Hutchinson, Esq., and others.

Anglo-Saxon Chronicle, (Rolls Series).

Bassano, Francis. Church Notes, (1710)

Bede, Venerable. Ecclesiastical History.

Bigsby, Rev. Robert. History of Repton, (1854).

Birch, W. de Gray. Memorials of St. Guthlac.

Browne, (Right Rev. Bishop of Bristol). Conversion of the Heptarchy.

Cox, Rev J. Charles. Churches of Derbyshire.

Derbyshire Archæological Journal, (1879—98).

Eckenstein, Miss Lina. Women under Monasticism.

Diocesan Histories, (S.P.C.K).

Dugdale. Monasticon.

Evesham, Chronicles of, (Rolls Series).

Gentleman's Magazine.

Glover, S. History of Derbyshire, (1829).

Green, J. R. Making of England.

Ingulph. History.

Leland. Collectanea.

Lingard. Anglo-Saxon Church.

Lysons. Magna Britannia, (Derbyshire), (1817).

Paris, Matthew. Chronicles, (Rolls Series).

Pilkington, J. " A View of the Present State of Derby-shire," (1789).

Repton Church Registers.

Repton School Register.

Searle, W. G. Onomasticon Anglo-Saxonicum.

Stebbing Shaw. History of Staffordshire.

        ,,   ,,   Topographer.

Tanner   Notitia Monastica.

CONTENTS.

LIST OF ILLUSTRATIONS.

CORRIGENDA.

Page 12.	*For*	Eaburgh	*read*	Eadburgh.
,,	14	,,	Ggga	,,	Egga
,,	74	,,	Solwey	,,	Solney.
,,	96	,,	Grindley	,,	Grinling.
,,	99	,,	preceptary	,,	preceptory.
,,	111.	,,	now	,,	father of the.
,.	115	,,	Bumaston	,,	Burnaston

Plate 2.

Repton Hall.

(Prior Overton's Tower, page 81.)

CHAPTER I.

REPTON (GENERAL).

REPTON is a village in the County of Derby, four miles east of Burton-on-Trent, seven miles south-west of Derby, and gives its name to the deanery, and with Gresley, forms the hundred, or division, to which it belongs.

The original settlers showed their wisdom when they selected the site: on the north flowed " the smug and silver Trent," providing them with water; whilst on the south, forests, which then, no doubt, extended in unbroken line from Sherwood to Charnwood, provided fuel; and, lying between, a belt of green pasturage provided fodder for cattle and sheep. The hand of time and man, has nearly destroyed the forests, leaving them such in name alone, and the remains of forests and pasturage have been " annexed." Repton *Common* still remains in name, in 1766 it was enclosed by Act of Parliament, and it and the woods round are no longer " common."

Excavations made in the Churchyard, and in the field to the west of it, have laid bare many foundations, and portions of Anglo-Saxon buildings, such as head-stones of doorways and windows, which prove that the site of the ancient Monastery, and perhaps the town, was on that part of the village now occupied by church, churchyard, vicarage and grounds, and was protected by the River Trent, a branch of which then, no doubt, flowed at the foot of its rocky bank. At some time unknown, the course of the river was interfered with. Somewhere,

A

above or about the present bridge at Willington, the river divided into two streams, one flowing as it does now, the other, by a very sinuous course, crossed the fields and flowed by the town, and so on till it rejoined the Trent above Twyford Ferry. Traces of this bed can be seen in the fields, and there are still three wide pools left which lie in the course of what is now called the "Old Trent."

There is an old tradition that this alteration was made by Hotspur. In Shakespeare's play of *Henry IV. Act III.* Hotspur, Worcester, Mortimer, and Glendower, are at the house of the Archdeacon at Bangor. A map of England and Wales is before them, which the Archdeacon has divided into three parts. Mortimer is made to say :

> " England, from Trent to Severn hitherto,
> By south and east is to my part assign'd :
> All westward, Wales beyond the Severn shore,
> And all the fertile land within that bound,
> To Owen Glendower ; and dear Coz, to you
> The remnant northward, lying off from Trent."

The "dear Coz" Hotspur, evidently displeased with his share, replies, pointing to the map ;—

> " Methinks my moiety, north from Burton here,
> In quantity equals not one of yours :
> See how this river comes me cranking in,
> And cuts me from the best of all my land,
> A huge half moon, a monstrous cantle out.
> *I'll have the current in this place damm'd up ;*
> *And here the snug and silver Trent shall run*
> *In a new channel fair and evenly :*
> *It shall not wind with such a deep indent,*
> *To rob me of so rich a bottom here."*

Whether this passage refers to the alteration of the course of the Trent at Repton, or not, we cannot say, but that it was altered is an undoubted fact. The dam can be traced just below the bridge, and on the Parish Map, the junction of the two is marked.

Pilkington in his History of Derbyshire refers to "eight acres of land *in an island betwixt Repton and Willington*" as belonging to the Canons of Repton Priory. They are still known as the Canons' Meadows. On this "island" is a curious parallelogram of raised earth, which is *supposed to be* the remains of a Roman Camp, called Repandunum by Stebbing-Shaw, O.R., the Historian of Staffordshire, but he gives no proofs for the assertion. Since the "Itineraries" neither mention nor mark it, its original makers must remain doubtful until excavations have been made on the spot. Its dimensions are, North side, 75 yards, 1 foot, South side, 68 yards, 1 foot, East side, 52 yards, 1 foot, West side, 54 yards, 2 feet. Within the four embankments are two rounded mounds, and parallel with the South side are two inner ramparts, only one parallel with the North. It is supposed by some to be "a sacred area surrounding tumuli." The local name for it is "The Buries." In my opinion it was raised and used by the Danes, who in A.D. 874 visited Repton, and destroyed it before they left in A.D. 875.

Before the Conquest the Manor of Repton belonged to Algar, Earl of Mercia. In Domesday Book it is described as belonging to him and the King, having a church and two priests, and two mills. It soon after belonged to the Earls of Chester, one of whom, Randulph de Blundeville, died in the year 1153. His widow, Matilda, with the consent of her son Hugh, founded Repton Priory.

In Lysons' *Magna Britannia*, we read, "The Capital Messuage of Repingdon was taken into the King's (Henry III.) hands in 1253." Afterwards it appears to have passed through many hands, John de Britannia, William de Clinton, Philip de Strelley, John Fynderne, etc., etc. In the reign of Henry IV., John Fynderne "was seised of an estate called the Manor of Repingdon *alias* Strelley's part," from whom it descended through George Fynderne to Jane Fynderne, who married Sir Richard Harpur, Judge of the Common Pleas, whose tomb is in the mortuary chapel of the Harpurs in Swarkeston Church. Round the alabaster slab of the tomb on which lie the effigies of Sir Richard and his wife, is the following inscription, "Here under were buryed the bodyes of Richard Harpur, one of the Justicies of the Comen Benche at Westminster, and Jane his wife, sister and heyer unto Thomas Fynderne of Fynderne, Esquyer. Cogita Mori." Since the dissolution of the Priory there have been two Manors of Repton, Repton Manor and Repton Priory Manor.

From Sir Richard Harpur the Manor of Repton descended to the present Baronet, Sir Vauncey Harpur-Crewe. Sir Henry Harpur, by royal license, assumed the name and arms of Crewe, in the year 1800.

The Manor of Repton Priory passed into the hands of the Thackers at the dissolution of the Priory, and remained in that family till the year 1728, when Mary Thacker devised it, and other estates, to Sir Robert Burdett of Foremark, Bart.

The Village consists of two main streets, which meet at the Cross Starting from the Church, in a southerly direction, one extends for about a mile, towards Bretby. The other, coming from Burton-on-Trent, proceeds in an easterly direction, through "Brook End," towards Milton, and Tickenhall, &c. The road from Willington was made in 1839, when it and the bridge were completed, and opened to the public. A swift stream, rising in the Pistern Hills, six miles to the south, runs through a broad valley, and used to turn four corn mills, (two of which are mentioned in Domesday Book,) now only two are worked, one at Bretby, the other at Repton. The first, called Glover's Mill, about a mile above Bretby, has the names of many of the Millers, who used to own or work it, cut, apparently, by their own hands, in the stone of which it is built. The last mill was the Priory Mill, and stood on the east side of the Priory, the arch, through which the mill-race ran, is still *in situ*, it was blocked, and the stream diverted to its present course, by Sir John Harpur in the year 1606. On the left bank of this stream, on the higher ground of the valley, the village has been built; no attempt at anything like uniformity of design, in shape or size, has been made, each owner and builder erected, house or cottage, according to his own idea or desire; these, with gardens and orchards, impart an air of quaint beauty to our village, whose inhabitants for centuries have been engaged, chiefly, in agriculture.   In the old Parish registers some of its inhabitants are described as "websters," and "tanners," but, owing to the growth of the trade in better situated towns, these trades gradually ceased.

During the Civil War the inhabitants of Repton and neighbourhood remained loyal and faithful to King Charles I. In 1642 Sir John Gell, commander of the Parliamentary forces stormed Bretby House, and in January, 1643, the inhabitants of Repton, and other parishes, sent a letter of remonstrance to the Mayor and Corporation of Derby, owing to the plundering excursions of soldiers under Sir John's command.   In the same year, Sir John Harpur's house, at Swarkeston, was stormed and taken by Sir John Gell.

In 1687 a wonderful skeleton, nine feet long! was discovered in a field, called Allen's Close, adjoining the churchyard of Repton, now part of the Vicarage grounds. The skeleton was in a stone coffin, with others to the number of one hundred arranged round it! During the year 1787 the grave was reopened, and a confused heap of bones was discovered, which were covered over with earth, and a sycamore tree, which is still flourishing, was planted to mark the spot.

During the present century few changes have been made in the village; most of them will be found recorded, either under chief events in the History of Repton, or in the chapters succeeding.

CHAPTER II.

REPTON (HISTORICAL).

THE PLACE-NAME REPTON, &c.

THE first mention of Repton occurs in the Anglo-Saxon Chronicle, under the year 755. Referring to "the slaughter" of King Ethelbald, King of Mercia, one out of the six MSS. relates that it happened "on Hreopandune," "at Repton"; the other five have "on Seccandune," "at Seckington," near Tamworth. Four of the MSS. spell the name "Hrepandune," one "Hreopadune," and one "Reopandune."

Under the year 874, when the Danes came from Lindsey, Lincolnshire, to Repton, "and there took winter quarters," four of the MSS. spell the name "Hreopedune," one "Hreopendune." Again, under the year 875, when they left, having destroyed the Abbey and the town, the name is spelt "Hreopedune." The final *e* represents the dative case. In Domesday Book it is spelt "Rapendune," "Rapendvne," or "Rapendvn." In later times, among the various ways of spelling the name, the following occur : — Hrypadun, Rypadun, Rapandun, Rapindon, Rependon, Repindon, Repingdon, Repyndon, Repington, Repyngton, Ripington, Rippington, &c., and finally Repton ; the final syllable *ton* being, of course, a corruption of the ancient *dun* or *don*.

Now as to the meaning of the name. There is no doubt about the suffix *dun*, which was adopted by the Anglo-Saxons from the Celts, and means *a hill*, and was

generally used to denote a hill-fortress, stronghold, or fortified place. As to the meaning of the prefix "Hreopan,"
"Hreopen," or "Repen," the following suggestions have
been made :—(1) "Hreopan" is the genitive case of a
Saxon proper name, "Hreopa," and means Hreopa's
hill, or hill-fortress. (2) "Hropan or Hreopan," a verb,
"to shout," or "proclaim"; or a noun, "Hrop,"
"clamour," or "proclamation," and so may mean "the
hill of shouting, clamour, or proclamation." (3) "Repan
or Ripan," a verb, "to reap"; or a noun, "Rep, or Rip,"
a harvest, "the hill of reaping or harvest." (4) "Hreppr,"
a Norse noun for "a village," "a village on a hill."
(5) "Ripa," a noun meaning "a bank," "a hill on a
bank," of the river Trent, which flows close to it.

The question is, which of these is the most probable
meaning ? The first three seem to suit the place and
position. It is a very common thing for a hill or place
to bear the name of the owner or occupier. As
Hreopandun was the capital of Mercia, many a council
may have been held, many a law may have been pro-
claimed, and many a fight may have been fought, with
noise and clamour, upon its hill, and, in peaceful times, a
harvest may have been reaped upon it, and the land
around. As regards the two last suggestions, the arrival
of the Norsemen, in the eighth century, would be too late
for them to name a place which had probably been in
existence, as an important town, for nearly two centuries
before they came.

The prefix "ripa" seems to favour a Roman origin,
but no proofs of a Roman occupation can be found. If
there are any, they lie hid beneath that oblong enclosure
in a field to the north of Repton, near the banks of the
river Trent, which Stebbing Shaw, in the *Topographer*
(Vol. II., p. 250), says "was an ancient colony of the
Romans called 'Repandunum.'" As the name does not
appear in any of the "Itineraries," nor in any of the
minor settlements or camps in Derbyshire, this statement
is extremely doubtful. Most probably the camp was
constructed by the Danes when they wintered there in

the year 874. The name Repandunum appears in Spruner and Menke's "Atlas Antiquus" as a town among the Cornavii (? Coritani), at the junction of the Trent and Dove !

So far as to its name. Now we will put together the various historical references to it.

"This place," writes Stebbing Shaw, (O.R.), in the *Topographer*, Vol. II., p. 250, "was an ancient colony of the Romans called Repandunum, and was afterwards called Repandun, (Hreopandum,) by the Saxons, being the head of the Mercian kingdom, several of their kings having palaces here."

"Here was, before A.D. 600, a noble monastery of religious men and women, under the government of an Abbess, after the Saxon Way, wherein several of the royal line were buried."

As no records of the monastery have been discovered we cannot tell where it was founded or by whom. Penda, the Pagan King of Mercia, was slain by Oswiu, king of Northumbria, at the battle of Winwadfield, in the year 656, and was succeeded by his son Peada who had been converted to Christianity, by Alfred brother of Oswiu, and was baptized, with all his attendants, by Finan, bishop of Lindisfarne, at Walton, in the year 632. (*Matt Paris, Chron. Maj.*) After Penda's death, Peada brought from the north, to convert Mercia, four priests, Adda, Betti, Cedda brother of St. Chad, and Diuma, who was consecrated first bishop of the Middle Angles and Mercians by Finan, but only ruled the see for two years, when he died and was buried " among the Middle Angles at Feppingum," which is supposed to be Repton. In the year 657 Peada was slain "in a very nefarious manner, during the festival of Easter, betrayed, as some say, by his wife," and was succeeded by his brother Wulphere.

Tanner, *Notitia*, f. 78 ; Leland, *Collect.*, Vol. II., p. 157 ; Dugdale, *Monasticon*, Vol. II., pp. 280—2, all agree that the monastery was founded before 660, so Peada, or his brother Wulphere could have been its founder.

The names of several of the Abbesses have been recorded. Eadburh, daughter of Ealdwulf, King of East Anglia. Ælfthryth (Ælfritha) who received Guthlac, (see p. 12). Wærburh (St. Werburgh) daughter of King Wulphere. Cynewaru (Kenewara) who in 835 granted the manor and lead mines of Wirksworth, on lease, to one Humbert.

Among those whom we know to have been buried within the monastery are Merewald, brother of Wulphere. Cyneheard, brother of the King of the West Saxons. Æthelbald, King of the Mercians, "slain at Seccandun (Seckington, near Tamworth), and his body lies at Hreopandun " (*Anglo-Saxon Chron.*) under date 755. Wiglaf or Withlaf, another King of Mercia, and his grandson Wistan (St. Wystan), murdered by his cousin Berfurt at Wistanstowe in 850 (see p. 15). After existing for over 200 years the monastery was destroyed by the Danes in the year 874. " In this year the army of the Danes went from Lindsey (Lincolnshire) to Hreopedun, and there took winter quarters," (*Anglo-Saxon Chron.*), and as Ingulph relates " utterly destroyed that most celebrated monastery, the most sacred mausoleum of all the Kings of Mercia."

For over two hundred years it lay in ruins, till, probably, the days of Edgar the Peaceable (958-75) when a church was built on the ruins, and dedicated to St. Wystan.

When Canute was King (1016-1035) he transferred the relics of St. Wystan to Evesham Abbey, where they rested till the year 1207, when, owing to the fall of the central tower which smashed the shrine and relics, a portion of them was granted to the Canons of Repton. (*see Life of St Wystan, p* 16.) In Domesday Book Repton is entered as having a Church with *two* priests, which proves the size and importance of the church and parish in those early times. Algar, Earl of Mercia, son of Leofric, and Godiva, was the owner then, but soon after, it passed into the hands of the King, eventually it was restored to the descendants of Algar, the Earls of Chester.

Matilda, widow of Randulph, Earl of Chester, with the consent of her son Hugh, enlarged the church, and founded the Priory, both of which she granted to the Canons of Calke, whom she transferred to Repton in the year 1172.

CHAPTER III.

REPTON'S SAINTS (GUTHLAC & WYSTAN).

" THE sober recital of historical fact is decked with legends of singular beauty, like artificial flowers adorning the solid fabric of the Church. Truth and fiction are so happily blended that we cannot wish such holy visions to be removed out of our sight," thus wrote Bishop Selwyn of the time when our Repton Saints lived, and in order that their memories may be kept green, the following account has been written.

ST. GUTHLAC.

At the command of Æthelbald, King of the Mercians, Felix, monk of Crowland, first bishop of the East Angles, wrote a life of St. Guthlac.

He derived his information from Wilfrid, abbot of Crowland, Cissa, a priest, and Beccelm, the companion of Guthlac, all of whom knew him.

Felix relates that Guthlac was born in the days of Æthelred, (675—704), his parents names were Icles and Tette, of royal descent. He was baptised and named Guthlac, which is said to mean " Gud-lac," " belli munus," " the gift of battle," in reference to the gift of one, destined to a military career, to the service of God. The sweet disposition of his youth is described, at length, by his biographer, also the choice of a military career, in which he spent nine years of his life. During those years he devastated cities and houses, castles and villages, with

fire and sword, and gathered together an immense
quantity of spoil, but he returned a third part of it to
those who owned it. One sleepless night, his conscience
awoke, the enormity of his crimes, and the doom awaiting
such a life, suddenly aroused him, at daybreak he
announced, to his companions, his intention of giving up
the predatory life of a soldier of fortune, and desired them
to choose another leader, in vain they tried to turn him
from his resolve, and so at the age of twenty-four, about
the year 694, he left them, and came to the Abbey of
Repton, and sought admission there. Ælfritha, the abbess,
admitted him, and, under her rule, he received the
"mystical tonsure of St. Peter, the prince of the Apostles."

For two years he applied himself to the study of sacred
and monastic literature.

The virtues of a hermit's life attracted him, and he
determined to adopt it, so, in the autumn of 696, he again
set out in search of a suitable place, and soon lost himself among the fens, not far from Gronta—which has
been indentified with Grantchester, near Cambridge—
here, a bystander, named Tatwine, mentioned a more
remote island named Crowland, which many had tried
to inhabit, but, owing to monsters, &c., had failed to do
so. Hither Guthlac and Tatwine set out in a punt, and,
landing on the island, built a hut over a hole made by
treasure seekers, in which Guthlac settled on St. Bartholomew's Day, (August 24th,) vowed to lead a hermit's
life. Many stories are related, by Felix, of his encounters
with evil spirits, who tried to turn him away from the
faith, or drive him away from their midst.

Of course the miraculous element abounds all through
the narrative, chiefly connected with his encounters with
evil spirits, whom he puts to flight, delivering those
possessed with them from their power. So great was
his fame, bishops, nobles, and kings, visit him, and
Ealburgh, Abbess of Repton, daughter of Aldulph, King
of East Angles, sent him a shroud, and a coffin of Derbyshire lead, for his burial, which took place on the 11th of
April, A.D. 714.

Such, in briefest outline, is the life of St. Guthlac.
Those who wish to know more about him, should consult
" The Memorials of St. Guthlac," edited by Walter de
Gray Birch. In it he has given a list of the manuscripts,
Anglo-Saxon, Latin, and Old English Verse, which
describe the Saint's life. He quotes specimens of all
of them, and gives the full text of Felix's life, with foot-
notes of various readings, &c., and, what is most interesting, has interleaved the life with illustrations, reproduced
by Autotype Photography, from the well known roll in
Harley Collection of MSS. in the British Museum. The
roll, of vellum, is nine feet long, by six inches and a half
wide, on it are depicted, in circular panels, eighteen
scenes from the life of the Saint. Drawn with " brown
or faded black ink, heightened with tints and transparent
colours, lightly sketched in with a hair pencil—in the
prevailing style of the twelfth century—the work of a
monk of Crowland, perhaps of the celebrated Ingulph,
the well known literary abbot of that monastery, it stands,
unique, in its place, as an example of the finest early
English style of freehand drawing," one or more of the
cartoons are missing.

The first cartoon, the left half of which is wanting, is
a picture of Guthlac and his companions asleep, clad in
chain armour.

The 2nd. Guthlac takes leave of his companions.

The 3rd. Guthlac is kneeling between bishop Headda,
and the abbess, in Repton abbey. The bishop is shearing
off Guthlac's hair.

The 4th. Guthlac, Tatwine, and an attendant are in a
boat with a sail, making their way back to the island of
Crowland.

The 5th. Guthlac, with two labourers, is building a
chapel.

The 6th. Guthlac, seated in the completed chapel,
receives a visit from an angel, and his patron saint
Bartholomew.

The 7th. Guthlac is borne aloft over the Chapel by five
demons, three of whom are beating him with triple-

thonged whips. Beccelm, his companion, is seated inside the Chapel, in front of the altar, on which is placed a chalice.

The 8th. Guthlac, with a nimbus of sanctity round his head, has been borne to the jaws of hell, (in which are a king, a bishop, and two priests) by the demons, and is rescued by St. Bartholomew, who gives a whip to Guthlac.

The 9th. The cell of Guthlac is surrounded by five demons, in various hideous shapes. He has seized one, and is administering a good thrashing with his whip.

The 10th. Guthlac expels a demon from the mouth of Ggga, a follower of the exiled Æthelbald.

The 11th. Guthlac, kneeling before bishop Headda, is ordained a priest.

The 12th. King Æthelbald visits Guthlac, both are seated, and Guthlac is speaking words of comfort to him.

The 13th. Guthlac is lying ill in his oratory, Beccelm is kneeling in front of him listening to his voice.

The 14th. Guthlac is dead, two angels are in attendance, one receiving the soul, "anima", as it issues from his mouth. A ray of light stretches from heaven down to the face of the saint.

The 15th. Beccelm and an attendant in a boat, into which Pega, sister of Guthlac, is stepping on her way to perform the obsequies of her brother.

The 16th. Guthlac, in his shroud, is being placed in a marble sarcophagus by Pega and three others, one of whom censes the remains.

The 17th. Guthlac appears to King Æthelbald.

The 18th. Before an altar stand thirteen principal benefactors of Crowland Abbey. Each one, beginning with King Æthelbald, carries a scroll on which is inscribed their name, and gift.

The Abbey of Crowland was built, and flourished till about the year 870, when the Danes burnt it down, four years later they destroyed Repton.

Guthlaxton Hundred in the southern part of Leicestershire, and four churches, dedicated to him, retain his name. The remains of a stone at Brotherhouse, bearing

his name, and a mouldering effigy, in its niche on the west
front of the ruins of Crowland Abbey, are still to be seen.
His "sanctus bell" was at Repton, and as we shall see,
in the account of the Priory, acquired curative powers for
headache.

ST. WYSTAN.

Among " the Chronicles and Memorials of Great
Britain and Ireland during the Middle Ages," published
by the authority of Her Majesty's Treasury, under the
direction of the Master of the Rolls is the "Chronicon
Abbatiæ de Evesham," written by Thomas de Marleberge
or Marlborough, Abbot of Evesham. In an appendix
to the Chronicle he also wrote a life of St. Wystan from
which the following facts, &c., have been gathered.

Wystan was the son of Winmund, son of Wiglaf, King
of Mercia, his mother's name was Elfleda. Winmund
died of dysentery during his father's life-time, and was
buried in Crowland Abbey, and, later on, his wife was
laid by his side. When the time came for Wystan to
succeed to the crown, he refused it, "wishing to become
an heir of a heavenly kingdom. Following the example
of his Lord and master, he refused an earthly crown,
exchanging it for a heavenly one," and committed the
kingdom to the care of his mother, and to the chief men
of the land. But his uncle Bertulph conspired against
him, "inflamed with a desire of ruling, and with a secret
love for the queen-regent." A council was assembled at
a place, known from that day to this, as Wistanstowe,
in Shropshire, and to it came Bertulph and his son
Berfurt. Beneath his cloak Berfurt had concealed a
sword, and (like Judas the traitor), whilst giving a kiss
of peace to Wystan, drew it and smote him with a
mortal wound on his head, and so, on the eve of Pente-
cost, in the year 849, "that holy martyr leaving his
precious body on the earth, bore his glorious soul to
heaven. The body was conveyed to the Abbey of
Repton, and buried in the mausoleum of his grandfather,

with well deserved honour, and the greatest reverence.
For thirty days a column of light, extending from the
spot where he was slain to the heavens above, was seen
by all those who dwelt there, and every year, on the day
of his martyrdom, the hairs of his head, severed by the
sword, sprung up like grass." Over the spot a church
was built to which pilgrims were wont to resort, to see
the annual growth of the hair.

The remains of St. Wystan rested at Repton till the
days of Canute (1016—1035), when he caused them to
be transferred to Evesham Abbey, " so that in a larger
and more worthy church the memory of the martyr might
be held more worthily and honourably." In the year
1207 the tower of Evesham Abbey fell, smashing the
presbytery and all it contained, including the shrine of
St. Wystan. The monks took the opportunity of inspect-
ing the relics, and to prove their genuineness, which
some doubted, subjected them to a trial by fire, the
broken bones were placed in it, and were taken out
unhurt and unstained. The Canons of Repton hearing
of the disaster caused by the falling tower, begged so
earnestly for a portion of the relics, that the Abbot
Randulph granted them a portion of the broken skull,
and a piece of an arm bone. The bearers of the sacred
relics to Repton were met by a procession of prior,
canons, and others, over a mile long, and with tears of
joy they placed them, " not as before in the mausoleum
of his grandfather, but in a shrine more worthy, more
suitable, and as honourable as it was possible to make
it," in their Priory church, where they remained till it
was dissolved in the year 1538.

In memory of St. Wystan, the first Parish Church of
Repton was dedicated to him, as we shall see in our
account of Repton Church.

Plate

Repton Church Crypt.

(Page 17.)

CHAPTER IV.

REPTON CHURCH.

EPTON CHURCH is built on the site of the Anglo-Saxon Monastery, which was destroyed by the Danes in the year 874. It was most probably built in the reign of Edgar the Peaceable (959—975), as Dr. Charles Cox writes :—" Probably about that period the religious ardour of the persecuted Saxons revived . . . . . their thoughts would naturally revert to the glories of monastic Repton in the days gone by." On the ruins of the " Abbey " they raised a church, and dedicated it to St. Wystan. According to several writers, it was built of stout oak beams and planks, on a foundation of stone, or its sides might have been made of wattle, composed of withy twigs, interlaced between the oak beams, daubed within and without with mud or clay. This church served for a considerable time, when it was re-built of stone. The floor of the chancel, supported on beams of wood, was higher than the present one, so the chancel had an upper and lower " choir," the lower one was lit by narrow lights, two of which, blocked up, can be seen in the south wall of the chancel. When the church was re-built the chancel floor was removed, and the lower " choir " was converted into the present *crypt*, by the introduction of a vaulted stone roof, which is supported by four spirally-wreathed piers, five feet apart, and five feet six inches high, and eight square responds, slightly fluted, of the same height, and distance apart, all with capitals with square abaci,

c

which are chamfered off below. Round the four walls
is a double string-course, below which the walls are
ashlar, remarkably smooth, as though produced by
rubbing the surface with stone, water and sand. The
vaulted roof springs from the upper string-course, the
ribs are square in section, one foot wide, there are no
diagonal groins, it is ten feet high, and is covered with
a thin coating of plaster, which is continued down to
the upper string-course. The piers are monoliths, and
between the wreaths exhibit that peculiar swell which
we see on the shafts of Anglo-Saxon belfry windows, &c.

The double string-course is terminated by the responds.
There were recesses in each of the walls of the crypt.
In the wall of the west recess there is a small arch,
opening into a smaller recess, about 18 inches square.
Many suggestions have been made about it : (1) it was a
"holy hole" for the reception of relics, (2) or a opening
in which a lamp could be kept lit, (3) or that it was used
as a kind of "hagioscope," through which the crypt could
be seen from the nave of the church, when the chancel
floor was higher, and the nave floor lower than they are
now.

There are two passages to the church, about two feet
wide and ten feet high, made from the western angles of
the crypt.

A doorway was made, on the north side, with steps
leading down to it, from the outside, during the
thirteenth century ; there is a holy water stoup in the
wall, on the right hand as you enter the door.

For many years it has been a matter of dispute how
far the recesses in the crypt, on the east, north, and south
sides, extended. Excavations just made (Sept. 1898),
have exposed the foundations of the recesses. The
recess on the south side is rectangular, not apsidal as
some supposed, it projects 2 ft. 2 in. from the surface of
the wall, outside, and is 6 ft. 2 in. wide. About two feet
below the ground level, two blocks of stone were discovered, (each 2 ft. × 1 ft. 4 in. × 1 ft. 9 in.), two feet
apart, they rest on a stone foundation. The inside

corners are chamfered off. On a level with the stone foundation, to the south of it, are two slabs under which a skeleton was seen, whose it was, of course, cannot be said. The present walls across the recesses, on the south and east, block them half up, and were built in later times.

The recess on the east end was destroyed when a flight of stone steps was made leading down to the crypt. These steps (there are six of them) are single, roughly made stones of varied length, resting on the earth, without mortar. When the flight was complete there would have been twelve, reaching from the top to the level of the crypt floor.

The steps would afford an easier and quicker approach to the crypt and church, but when they were made cannot now be said.

The recess on the north side was also destroyed when the outer stairway, and door, were placed there, probably, as before stated, in the thirteenth century. On the outside surface of the three walls, above the ground level, are still to be seen traces of the old triangular-shaped roofs which covered the three recesses, and served as buttresses to the walls. Similar "triangular arches" are to be seen at Barnack, and Brigstock.

The eastern end of the north aisle is the only portion of the ancient transepts above the ground level. During the restorations in 1886 the foundations of the Anglo-Saxon nave were laid bare, they extend westward up to and include the base of the second pier; the return of the west-end walls was also discovered, extending about four feet inwards.

Over the chancel arch the removal of many coats of whitewash revealed an opening, with jambs consisting of long and short work; a similar opening to the north of it used to exist, it is now blocked up.

The *Early English Style* is only represented by foundations laid bare during the restoration in 1885, and now indicated in the north and south aisles, by parallel lines of the wooden blocks, with which the church is paved.

In the south aisle the foundations of a south door were also discovered (see plan of church). To this period belong the windows in the north side of the chancel, and in the narrow piece of wall between the last arch and chancel wall on the north side of the present choir. There were two corresponding windows on the south side, one of which remains. All these windows have been blocked up.

The *Decorated Style* is represented in the nave by four out of the six lofty pointed arches, supported by hexagonal columns; the two, on either side, at the east end of the nave, were erected in the year 1854.

The tower and steeple were finished in the year 1340. Basano, in his Church Notes, records the fact—" An⁰ 1320 ?40. The tower steeple belonging to the Prior's Church of this town was finished and built up, as appears by a Scrole in Lead, having on it these words—" Turris adaptatur qua traiectū decoratur. M c ter xx bis. Testu Palini Johis."

A groined roof of stone, having a central aperture, through which the bells can be raised and lowered, separates the lower part of the tower from the belfry.

The north and south aisles were extended to the present width. The eastern end of the south aisle was also enlarged several feet to the south and east, and formed a chapel or chantry, as some say, for the Fyndernes, who were at one time Lords of the Repton Manor. A similar, but smaller, chapel was at the east end of the north aisle, and belonged to the Thacker family. They were known as the " Sleepy Quire," and the " Thacker's Quire." Up to the year 1792 they were separated by walls (which had probably taken the place of carved screens of wood) in order to make them more comfortable, and less draughty! These walls were removed in 1792, when " a restoration " took place.

The square-headed south window of the " Fynderne Chapel " composed of four lights, with two rows of trefoil and quatrefoil tracery in its upper part, is worthy of notice as a good specimen of this style, and was

probably inserted about the time of the completion of the
tower and spire. The other windows in the church of
one, two, three, and four lights, are very simple examples
of this period, and, like the chancel arch, have very little
pretensions to architectural merit, in design at least.

The *Perpendicular Style* is represented by the clerestory
windows of two lights each, the roof of the church, and
the south porch.

The high-pitched roof of the earlier church was lowered
—the pitch is still indicated by the string-course on the
eastern face of the tower—the walls over the arcades
were raised several feet from the string-course above the
arches, and the present roof placed thereon. It is supported by eight tie-beams, with ornamented spandrels
beneath, and wall pieces which rest on semi-circular
corbels on the north side, and semi-octagonal corbels
on the south side. The space above the tie-beams, and
the principal rafters is filled with open work tracery.
Between the beams the roof is divided into six squares
with bosses of foliage at the intersections of the rafters.

The south porch, with its high pitched roof, and vestry,
belongs to this period. It had a window on either side,
and was reached from the south aisle by a spiral staircase
(see plan of church).

The *Debased Style* began, at Repton, during the year
1719, and ended about the year 1854. In the year 1719
a singers' gallery was erected at the west end of the
church, and the arch there was bricked up.

In the year 1779 the crypt was " discovered " in a
curious way. Dr. Prior, Headmaster of Repton School,
died on June 16th of that year, a grave was being made
in the chancel, when the grave-digger suddenly disappeared
from sight : he had dug through the vaulted roof, and so
fell into the crypt below ! In the south-west division of
the groined roof, a rough lot of rubble, used to mend the
hole, indicates the spot.

During the year 1792 " a restoration " of the church
took place, the church was re-pewed, in the " horse-box "
style! All the beautifully carved oak work " on pews

and elsewhere" which Stebbing Shaw describes in the
Topographer (May, 1790), and many monuments were
cleared out, or destroyed. Some of the carved oak found
its way into private hands, and was used to panel a
dining-room, and a summer-house. Some of the carved
panels have been recovered, and can be seen in the vestry
over the south porch. One of the monuments which used
to be on the top of an altar tomb " at the upper end of
the north aisle," was placed in the crypt, where it still
waits a more suitable resting-place. It is an effigy of a
Knight in plate armour (circa Edward III.), and is
supposed to be Sir Robert Francis, son of John Francis,
of Tickenhall, who settled at Foremark. If so, Sir
Robert was the Knight who, with Sir Alured de Solney,
came to the rescue of Bishop Stretton in 1364, and is an
ancestor of the Burdetts, of Foremark.

The crypt seems to have been used as a receptacle for
" all and various " kinds of " rubbish " during the restoration, for, in the year 1802, Dr. Sleath found it nearly
filled up, as high as the capitals, with portions of ancient
monuments, grave-stones, &c., &c. In the corner,
formed by north side of the chancel and east wall of the
north aisle, a charnel, bone, or limehouse had been placed
in the Middle Ages : this house was being cleaned out by
Dr. Sleath's orders, when the workmen came upon the
stone steps leading down to the crypt, following them
down they found the doorway, blocked up by " rubbish,"
this they removed, and restored the crypt as it is at the
present day.

During the years 1842 and 1848 galleries in the north
and south aisles, extending from the west as far as the
third pillars, were erected.

In 1854, the two round arches and pillars, on either
side of the eastern end of the nave, were removed, and
were replaced by the present pointed arches and
hexagonal piers, for, as before stated, the sake of
uniformity ! Thus an interesting portion belonging to
the ancient church was destroyed. The illustration
opposite was copied from a drawing done, in the year

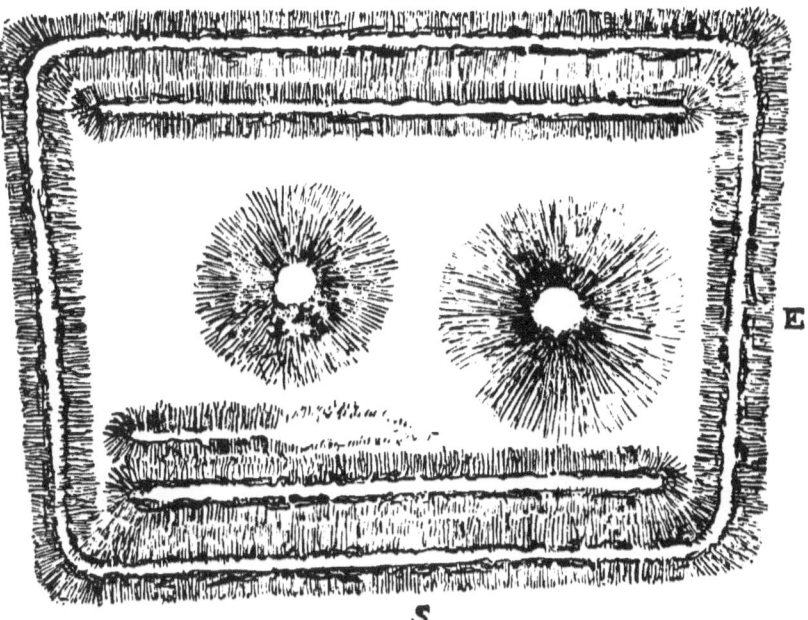

N.

E.

S.

Repton Camp.

(F. C. H.)   (Page 3.)

Plate 4.

Repton   Church.

(Before 1854.)   (Page 22.)

1847, by G. M. Gorham, then a pupil in the school, now Vicar of Masham, Bedale. To him our thanks are due for allowing me to copy it. It shows what the church was like in his time, 1847.

In 1885 the last restoration was made, when the Rev. George Woodyatt was Vicar. The walls were scraped, layers of whitewash were removed, the pews, galleries, &c., were removed, the floor of the nave lowered to its proper level, a choir was formed by raising the floor two steps, as far west as the second pier, the organ was placed in the chantry at the east end of the south aisle. The floor of nave and aisles was paved with wooden blocks, the choir with encaustic tiles. The whole church was re-pewed with oak pews, and "the choir" with stalls, and two prayer desks. A new pulpit was given in memory of the Rev. W. Williams, who died in 1882. The " Perpendicular roof " was restored to its original design : fortunately there was enough of the old work left to serve as models for the repair of the bosses, &c. The clerestory windows on the south side were filled with " Cathedral " glass. The splendid arch at the west end was opened.

The base of the old font was found among the *débris*, a new font, designed by Sir Arthur Blomfield, (the architect employed to do the restoration), was fixed on it, and erected under the tower.

Since that restoration, stained glass windows have been placed in all the windows of the north aisle by Messrs. James Powell and Sons, Whitefriars Glass Works, London ; the one in the south aisle is also by them. The outside appearance of the church roof was improved by the addition of an embattled parapet, the roof itself was recovered with lead.

In 1896 all the bells were taken down, by Messrs. John Taylor, of Loughborough, and were thoroughly examined and cleansed, two of them, the 5th and 6th (the tenor bell), were re-cast, (see chapter on Bells).

The only part of the church not restored is the chancel, and we hope that the Lord of the Manor, Sir Vauncey

Harpur-Crewe, Bart., will, some day, give orders for its careful, and necessary restoration.

INCUMBENTS, &c. OF REPTON.

	Jo. Wallin, curate. Temp. Ed. VI.
1584	Richard Newton, curate.
1602	Thomas Blandee, B.A., curate.
,,	John Horobine
1612	George Ward, minister
	Mathew Rodgers, minister
1648	Bernard Fleshuier, ,,
1649	George Roades, ,,
1661	John Robinson, ,,
1663	John Thacker, M.A., minister.
.,	William Weely, curate.
1739	Lowe Hurt, M.A.
1741	William Astley, M.A.
1742	John Edwards, B.A.
1804	John Pattinson.
1843-56	Joseph Jones, M.A.
1857-82	W. Williams.
1883-97	G. Woodyatt, B.A.
1898	A. A. McMaster, M.A.

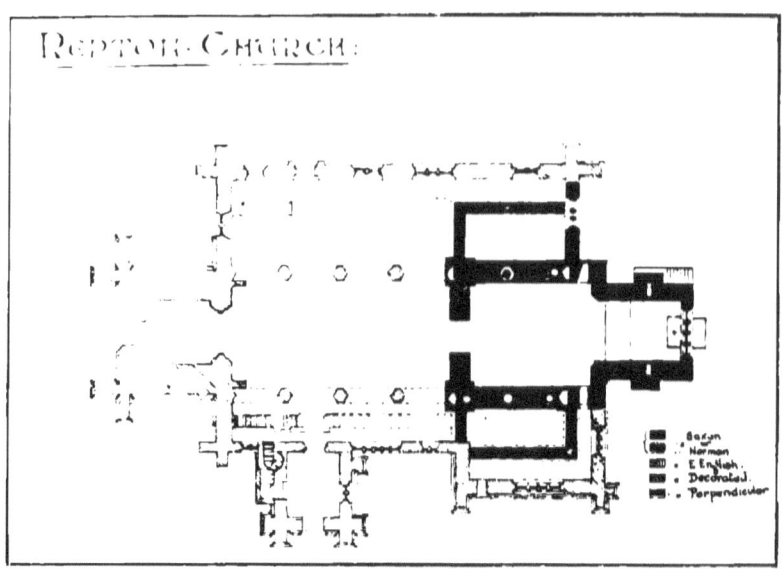

Plan of Repton Church

(F. C. H.)

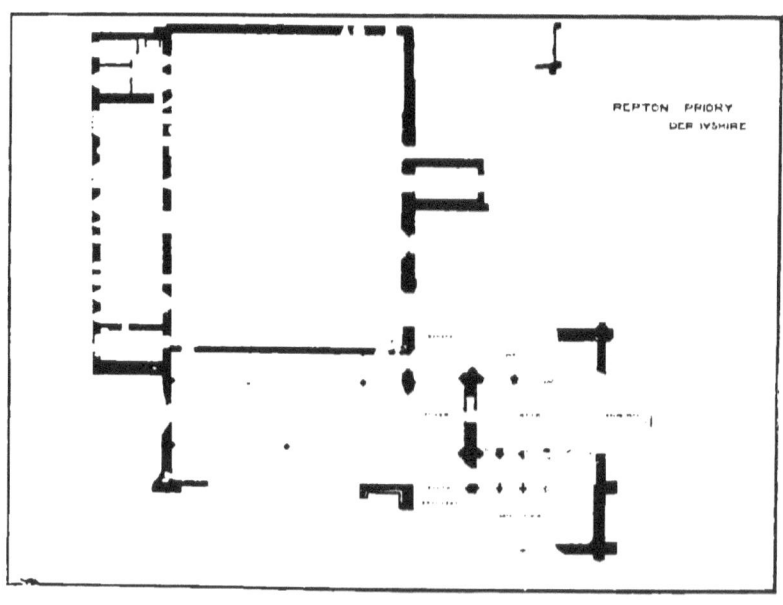

Plate 5.

Plan of Repton Priory.

(W. H. H. ST. JOHN HOPE, Mens et Del.)

(Page 25.)

CHAPTER V.

REPTON CHURCH REGISTERS.

HERE are three ancient register books of births, baptisms, marriages and burials, and one register book of the Churchwardens' and Constables' Accounts of the Parish of Repton. They extend from 1580 to 1670.

The oldest Volume extends from 1580 to 1629: the second from 1629 to 1655: the third from 1655—1670. The Churchwardens' and Constables' Accounts from 1582 to 1635.

The oldest Volume is a small folio of parchment (13 in. by 5 in.) of 45 leaves, bound very badly, time-stained and worn, in parts very badly kept, some of the leaves are loose, and some are quite illegible. It is divided into two parts, the first part (of thirty pages) begins with the year 1590 and extends to 1629: the second part begins with "Here followeth the register book for Ingleby, formemarke and Bretbye," from 1580 to 1624.

The Second Volume consists of eighteen leaves of parchment (13 in. by 6 in.), unbound, the entries are very faded, only parts of them are legible, they extend from 1629 to 1655.

The Third Volume has twenty-six leaves (11½ in. by 5½ in.). The entries are very legible, and extend from 1655 to 1670.

D

On the first page is written :

December yᵉ 31, 1655.

Geo: Roades yᵉ day & yeare above written approved & sworne Register for yᵉ parrish of Repton in yᵉ County of Derby   By me JAMES ABNEY.

THE FOLLOWING ENTRIES OCCUR.

1595   Milton. Wᵐ Alt who was drowned buried yᵉ 26 of ffebruarie.

1604   William a poor child wh died in the Church Porch buried yᵉ 4th of June.

1610   Mʳᵉˢ Jane Thacker daughter of Mr Gilbert Thacker Esquyer buryed the Xth of January Aº Dmi 1610.

"Vixit Jana deo, vivet pia Jana supernis, Esto Panôphæo gratia grata Iovi."

1612   Mʳ Gilbert Thacker Esquyer buryed the X of July.

1613   John Wayte churchⁿ entered the XXVI of Aprill.

1638   Philip yᵉ sonne of Mʳ Haughton & Lady Sarah his wife was baptᵗ at Bratby. March 30.

1638   The lady Jane Burdit wife of Sᶦʳ Thomas Burdit buryed the 24th of March.

1640   Robert the sonne of Mʳ Francis Burdet of Formark Esquiour was borne the 11th day of January and baptized the 4th day of February 1640.

1647   William the son of Will Bull bap about Candlemas.

1648   John Wilkinson of Englebye was bur Nov 4. Recᵈ 6/8 for the grave.

1650   Godfrey Thacker sen burᵈ March 26th.

1652   Old Ashe of Milton bur Oct 12.

1657   Samuel yᵉ son of Thomas Shaw yᵉ younger bap 28 June.

(He became the eminent Nonconformist Divine &c.)

1657   A *tabler* at Tho Bramly bur Aug :

(*Tabler*, a pupil of Repton School who lodged or *tabled* in the village).

1658   Y^e foole at Anchorchurch bur Aprill 19.

1658   James a poore man dyed at Bretby Manner was bur May 20.

1660   A ladd of Nuball's of Engleby bur ye same day Jan : 2.

1664   Mr Thomas Whitehead was bur Oct 17.
       (1st Ussher of Repton School.)

1666   Thos Rathban (Rathbone) the Under School-master was bur Nov 30.

1667   Mr William Ullock the Head Schoolmaster of Repton School died May the 13° and was buried in the Chancel May the 15°.

Collected at Repton (for reliefe of ye inhabitants of Soulbay in ye County of Suffolk y^t suffered by fire) October ye 30 1659 the sume of Tenn shillings and eight pence.

GEO : ROADES, Pastor.

Several similar collections, " for the fire att Wytham Church, Sussex, the sume of 3s. 6d."

Sep^t 4 1664 " Towards the repairs of the church at Basing in the county of Southampton 4s. 3d."

Feb. 19 1664 " For the inhabitants of Cromer at Shipden ye sume of four shillings five pence."

" For two widdows that came with a letter of request viz : Mrs Elizabeth Benningfield and Mrs Mary Berry the sum of 3s. 4d."

Ditto for Mrs Calligane 3s. 2d.

Sepr 23 1660 " For a fire att Willinghal Staffordshire ye sum of 13/s."

GEO : ROADES, Minister.
JOHN STONE, Churchwardens.
his ✠ mark.

Across the last page of the register is written this sage piece of advice :

" Beware toe whome you doe commit the secrites of your mind for fules in fury will tell all moveing in there minds."

RICHARD ROGERSON, 1684.

NAMES OF REPTON FAMILIES IN REGISTERS.

Pickeringe, Pyckering.
Meykyn, Meakin, Meakyn, Meakine, Meykyn.
Orchard.
Byshopp, Bushopp.
Cautrill or ell.
Measam, Measom, Meysom, Mesam, Mesom,
Messam, Measome, Meysum, Measham, Meysham.
Gamble, Gambell.
Ratcliffe, Ratleif.
Waite, Weat, Wayte, Weyte, Weite, Weayt.
Marbury, Marburie, Marberrow.
Keelinge.
Wayne.
Gilbert.
Nubould, Nuball.
Chedle, Chetle, Chetill.
Bancrafte, Banchroft.
Thacker or Thackquer.
Guddall.
Myminge, Meming, Mimings.
Gudwine, Goodwine.
Bull.
Eyton, Eaton, Eton.
Drowborrow.
Dowglast.
Bladonne. Blaidon. (carrier.)
Dakin. Dakyn.
Wainewrigh, Waynewright.
Rivett, Ryvett, Rivet.
Kynton.
Heawood.
Budworth.
Mariyott.
Pratt.
Smith als Hatmaker.
Bykar.
Ward.

Nicholas, Birchar.
Bolesse.
Shaw.
Heardwere.
Stanlye.
Chaplin, Charpline, Chaplayne.
Myrchell.
Bowlayes.
Fairebright.
Hygate.
Denyse, Deonys.
Heiginbotham, Higginbottom
Shortose, Shorthasse
Howlebutt.
Wixon Wigson
Waudall or ell.
Morleigh
Hastings Crowborough, or Croboro, Crobery, Cro-barrow.
Damnes. (2nd usher of school)
Boakes, Boaks.
Proudman.
Bakster.
Chauntry, Chautry.
Ebbs.
Wallace
Sault.
Bastwicke.
Hooton.
Truelove
Gressley, Greasley.
Pegg.
Jurdan.
Ilsly.
Robards.
Steeviston of Milton
Rathbone, Rathban. (under schoolmaster.)
Poisar.
Nuton.

Dixeson.

Doxy

The Register book of the Churchwardens' and Constable's Accounts extends from 1582 to 1635, and includes Repton, and the Chapelries of Formark, Ingleby, and Bretby.

It is a narrow folio volume of course paper, (16 in. by 6 in., by 2 in. thick), and is bound with a parchment which formed part of a Latin Breviary or Office Book, with music and words. The initial letters are illuminated, the colours, inside, are still bright and distinct.

At the beginning of each year the accounts are headed "Compotus gardianorum Pochialis Eccle de Reppindon," then follow :

(1) The names of the Churchwardens and Constable for the year.

(2) The money (taxes, &c.,) paid by the Chapelries above mentioned.

(3) The names and amounts paid by Tenants of Parish land.

(4) Money paid by the Parish to the Constable.

(5) Money "gathered for a communion," 1st mentioned in the year 1596. At first it was gathered only once in July, but afterwards in January, June, September, October, and November.

The amounts vary from jd to vjd.

(6) The various "items" expended by the Churchwardens and Constable.

Dr. J. Charles Cox examined the contents of the Parish Chest, and published an account of the Registers &c., and accounts, in Vol. I. of the Journal of the Derbyshire Archæological Society, 1879. Of the Accounts he writes, "it is the earliest record of parish accounts, with the exception of All Saints', Derby, in the county," and "the volume is worthy of a closer analysis than that for which space can now be found." Acting on that hint, during the winter months of 1893-4, I made most copious extracts from the Accounts, and also a "verbatim et literatim " transcript of the three registers, which I hope will be published some day.

Dr. Cox's article is most helpful in explaining many obsolete words, curious expressions, customs, and references to events long ago forgotton, a *few* of the thousands of entries are given below :

The first five leaves are torn, the entries are very faded and illegible.

1582	It for kepyng the clocke	ixs
1583	It to the glacyier for acct whole year	vjs viijd
	It to the Constable for his wages	iiijs
	(Several references to the bells which will be found in the chapter on the bells.)	
	It to the ryngers the xviith day of November	xijd
	(Accession to Queen Elizabeth.)	
	It to John Colman for kylling two foxes	xijd
	(A similar entry occurs very frequently.)	
1584	It for a boke of Artycles	vjd
	(Issued by order of Archbishop Whitgift, called the " Three Articles.")	
	It for washying the surplis	viijd
1585	It Layed for the at the Visitatun at Duffeyld	ijs vjd
	It for wyne the Saturday before Candlemas day for the Communion. (*Candlemas day*, or Purification of the B. Virgin Mary, when *candles* used to be carried in procession.)	vs
	It for bread	vjd
	It at the Vysitation at Repton	ijs viijd
1586	It at my lord byshopps vysitation at Darby spent by the Churwardens and sidemen	vs
	It of *our ladies even*, given to the ringers for the preservation (ot) our Queene	xijd
	(*Our ladies even*, eve of the Annunciation of the B. Virgin Mary. *Preservation*	

of *our Queene*, from the Babington conspiracy.)

1587 It to Gylbarte Hynton for pavynge the
    Church floore   iijli iijs jd

A note of the armoure of Repton given into.

1590 the hands of Richard Weatte, beyinge
    Constable Anno Di 1590 Inprimis ij
    corsletts w^t all that belongeth unto
    them.

It ij platt cotts (coats of plate armour.)

It ij two sweordes, iij dagers, ij gyrgells (girdles).

It ij calivers wth flaxes and tuchboxe.

(*calivers*, *flaxes*, muskets, flasks for powder, *touch boxes* to hold the priming powder.)

It ij pycks and ij halberds.

It for the Treband Souldear a cote and bowe and a scheffe of arrows, and a quiver and a bowe.

(*Treband Souldear* == our volunteer. Train-band soldiers were formed in 1588, to oppose the Spanish Armada.)

It to Mr. Heawoode for the Comen
    praer boke   ixs

It geven to Mr. Heawoode for takynge }
    payne in gatheryng tythyne   }   xvjd

1592 It geven to Rycharde Prince for Recevy- }
    inge the bull and lokinge to hym   }   jd

1594 It spent at Darby when I payde the
    money for the lame soldiars (returned
    from France.)   iiijd

1595 It spente at Darby when we weare called }
    by sytatyon xxiii daye of January   }   vjs viijd

It geven to Thomas Belsher for bryngy- }
    ing a sertyfycatte for us beying }   viijd
    excommunycatt   }

(Excommunication issued by the Arch-

deacon owing to the neglect of the
Church windows.)

It spent att Darby—where we weare }
called by Sytation for glazing the }   xxd
Church—in the court }

It at Darby when we sartyfyed that our }   viijd
Church was glazed—to the Regester }

1596   In this year the amt "gathered for a
communion," is first mentioned.
The amounts varied from jd to vjd.

Also an account of "a dowble tythyne
levied and gathered for ye Church
by Gilbart Hide, at ijd per head, on
all beasts &c. in Repton and Milton.

1598   It payd to Will Orchard for ye meaned }   iiijs iiijd
souldyers for ye whole yeare }

(By an act passed, 35 Eliz. cap. 4. the
relief of *maimed* soldiers, and sailors
was placed on the parochial assess-
ments.)

It payd to Willm Massye for killinge of }   iijs
towe baggers (badgers) and one foxe }

1600   It payd to the parritor (*apparitor*, an
officer of the Archdeacon's court.)   vd

1601   " The Constables charges this p'sent
yeare 1601.

Spent at ye muster at Stapenhill ye xxi
day of Decr   xvd

It payd to ye gealle (jail) for ye halfe
yeare   vjs viijd

It spent ye v daye of Aprill at ye leat
(court)   viijd

It for mending ye pinfould in Pinfold
Lane)   iiijd

It for mendinge ye stockes and for
wood for them   xjd

(The *stocks* used to stand in front of the
village cross.)

E

It pay^d to Mr. Coxe for a p'cept for
Watchinge & Wardinge   iiijd

("*Watchinge & Wardinge.*" A term
used to imply the duties of Parish
Constables. The number of men
who were bound to keep *watch and
ward*, &c., is specified in the statute
of Winchester (13 ed. I.).

It given to ye prest sowldiers   xijd

It was in the year 1601 that the conspiracy of Essex, in which the Earl
of Rutland was implicated, was discovered. Special arrangements were
made to meet it. A general muster
of (*pressed*) soldiers was made in
Derbyshire.

It pay^d for one sworde   iiijs
It ,, ,, 3 girdles   iijs
It ,, ,, dressing ye pikes   vjd
It ,, ,, one le(a)thering for ye flaxe   vjd
It ,, ,, dagger sheathe, & a sworde
scaber   xijd
It pay^d for one horse to carry ye armor }
and for bringing it home }   xiijd
It pay^d for a payre of Mouldes (for
making bullets)   viijd
It spent ledinge ye armore to Darbey   xijd
(According to the Statute of Win-
chester the armour had to be taken
by the constables to be viewed.)

It spent wth ye saltpeter men   ijd

("*Saltpeter men*" engaged during the
reign of James I. and Charles I. in
collecting animal fluids, which were
converted in saltpetre, and used in
the manufacture of gunpowder.)

It spent wth a prisoner being w'h him }
all night and going with him to Darbye }   iiijs   ijd

It pay^d to Thomas Pearson for mend- } xjs iiijd
   ing the crosse   }
        (The Village Cross.)

1602 It given to gipsies ye XXX of Januarye
     to avoid ye towne   xxd
     ("This is by far the earliest mention
     of gypsies in the Midland Counties."
     They arrived in England about 1500,
     in 1530 they were forbidden to
     wander about, and were ordered to
     leave the country.)

It pay^d in the offishalles Courte takinge } viijd
   our othes.   }
(The *oaths* in taking office as Church-
     wardens.)

It pay^d to ye Clarke of ye Markett for
     a proclamatione   vjd

It pay^d to Thos Chamberlain for kill-
     inge of vii hedgehoges   vjd

It rec^d by these Churchwardens Henry
     Pratt s^r, John Cartter, Henry Caut-
     rall, Thos Hill the daye and yeare
     above say^d (xviii Dec 1603) One
     boxe wth xviii pieces of evidences.
(*Evidences* = deeds referring to plots
     of land, &c., in, or near the Parish.
     There are 17 of these deeds in the
     church chest.)
The Chalice.
One olde boxe with a cheane thereto
     fixed, towe pieces of leade and four
     Keayes.

1603 It spent in makinge a search the night
     the robbery was done in Caulke   iijd

1604 It pay^d for wine for a Communione
     ye xiij daye of January for 3 gallands   iiijs
     It for bread   ijd
     Firste spent at ye metinge about
     Geneva   iiijd

	It spent goinge to Darbye to paye ye money for Geneva	vjd		

It spent goinge to Darbye to paye y^e
money for Geneva   vjd
(A collection for the support of refugees
there.)

It pay^d for one booke of ye constitu-
tion of o^r Kinge   xxd
(Issued by order of King James after
the Hampton Court Conference.)

1605   It pay^d for one booke of thanksgivinge
for our Kinge   vjd
(After the Gunpowder Plot.)

1609   It given to the parritor from the
bishop *(sic)* of Canterbury   xijd
It payde for poyntinge the steeple   vli   o   o

1610   It Receaved of the Churchwardens of
Bretbye for there part towards byinge   iijs
the booke of Jewells workes

1611   It spent the Ambulatione weeke   ijs
(Perambulating the parish, or "beating
the bounds" in Rogation week.)
For ledinge corne to the tithe barne
(which amounted to)   vli iiijs xjd
For gatheringe of tithe for Mr Burdane
19 days & half   jli ixs iijd
5   „   „   „
without his mare   vjs vd

_____
jli xvs viijd

1614   It given uppon Candellmas daye to
one that made a sermone   ijs

The Church Bookes.

First one Bible.

2 bookes of Common Prayer.

One booke of Paraphase of Erasmus uppon the
Gospells.

The Contraversye betwyxte Whittegifte and Cartt-
righte, Jowell and Harrddinge.

The booke of Jewells workes.

3 prayer bookes.

The booke of the queens Injunctions.

One booke of Sermons.

One booke of Articles had at the Bishopes visitatione.

The said bookes be in the Keepinge of Mr. Watts-sone (Headmaster of Repton School, 1594—1621), except the Bible and one booke of Common Prayer.

1615 A long list of 77 subscribers for "a
      newe beell." Probably the VIth bell
      (the tenor). Sum gathered   xijli viijs viijd

1616 Receaved by Christopher Ward, Constable, from
      John Cantrell, the Townes Armore.

      2 Corsletts with 2 pickes.

      2 Culivers—(guns).

      One flaske and tuchboxe.

      V head peeces ; towe of them ould ones.

      2 howllboardes.

      One payre of Banddebrowes.

      (Small wooden or tin cases, covered with leather,
      each holding one charge for musket or culiver,
      fastened to a broad band of leather, called a
      bandoleer, worn over the shoulder).

      2 oulde girdles.

      3 newe girdles : twoe of them with the sowldiers.

      3 payre of hanggers in the sowldiers keepinge.

      3 sowrdes, with two daggers.

      Allsoe the swordes in sowldiers keepinge.

      Allsoe 2 platte Coottes yt Clocksmith not delivered.

      It paid for an Admonitione here and
      there to enter into matrimonie agree- } vjd
      able to the lawe

1617 It given in ernest for a newe byble   xijd
      Receaved for the ould Byble   vs

1618 It paide for a Newe Byble   xliijs
      (This Bible is still in the Parish chest, in a very
      good state of preservation. "Imprinted at
      London by Robert Barker, Printer to the Kings
      most Excellent Majestie. Anno 1617.")

It paid for a the Common Prayer booke   viijs

1619 It paid to Rich. Meashame for Killing
of vii hedghoges   vjd

1621 A list of the church books, as above, "delivered
unto the saide churchwardens Willm Meakine,
Tho Gill, Edward Farmour."

1622 Bookes sent to Mr Willm Bladone to be emploied
for the use of the Parrish, and to be disposed of
at the discretione of Mr Thomas Whiteheade
(Headmaster of Repton School, 1621—1639).
Rec^d by Mr Robert Kellett, Godfry Cautrell,
Roger Bishope, and Robert Orchard, Churchwardens 1622, the XXVth of December, the
said bookes, videlicet : —

First a faire Bible well bound and hinged.

2. Bp Babingtone his worckes.

3. Mr Elton on the Collosians.

4. Mr Perkins on the Creede.

5. Mr Dod and Cleaver on ye Commandments.

6. Bellinging(Bellynny)(Belamy) his Catechesmie.

7. Mr Yonge his Househould Govermente.

8. The first and second partte of the true watche.

9. The second partte of the said true watche by
Mr Brinsley.

10. The plaine mane's pathewaye, and sermon of
Repenttance written by Mr Dentte.

11. Bradshawe's p'paracon (preparation) to ye Re-
ceavinge of ye Bodie and bloude.

12. Hieron his Helpe to Devotione.

13 and 14. Allsoe towe bookes of Martters (Fox's).

15. Dowenams worckes.

The conditions to be observed concerning the
usinge and lendinge of the forsaid bookes.

First that the said minister nowe p'sent and
Churchwardens and all theire successors shall
yearely at the accountt daye for the parrish
deliver up the bookes to be viewed by
Mr Whiteheade wth the parrishioners.

Allsoe that the said minister and churchwardens
or any one of them shall have authoritie to lend
any of the said bookes to any of the parrish of
Reptonne for the space of one, 2 or 3 months,
as they in there discretione shall see fittinge,
one this condicione, that the parties borrowinge
anye of the bookes aforenamed eyther fowly
bruisinge tearinge defaceinge or embezellinge
the said bookes borrowed, shall make good the
said bookes thus defaced, towrne, bruised, or
embezelled unto the parrish.

Allsoe that the said bookes, kept by the minister
and Churchwarddens in some convenient place
shall not be lent more than one at a time to
anye of the parish.

Allsoe that anye p'son borrowinge any of the
said bookes shall subscribe his name on borrowinge of the same booke.

(Allsoe the name) of every booke by anye
borrowed shall (be entered) by the said
minister and churchwarddens.

(This is a list, and rules of the first "lending
library" mentioned in Derbyshire. The books
have been " embezelled " years ago.)

1623 It given to the Ringers at the time of Prince
Charlles his comminge forth of Spaine.
(When he and Buckingham went to Madrid, to
arrange a marriage with the Infanta of Spain.)

1625 It paide for towe bookes appoyntted }
for prayer and fastinge   }   xxd

1626 Paid for a linnen bagge to keepe the }
Chalice with the cover   }   ijd

It paid for a booke of Thanksgiving   xiijd

1627 It spent in takinge down the Clocke   xijd
It paid for makinge the Clocke   iijli
It paid for carryinge the Clocke to }
Ashby and fetchinge yt againe   } iijs

1628 It given unto a preacher the Sabboth }
daye beinge the 30ᵗʰ of December } iiijs

	It paide for a littell prayer book	iijd
1629	It given ye 24th of May to a preacher	iijs ivd
1630	It paide for towe excommunicacions	xvjd
	It paide the IXth of November for the Retanene of excommunicacions	ijs
1632	It spent the VIth daye of May going the Ambulacione	ijs ivd

Delivered to Gilbt Weatt, John Pratt, Church-wardens, the 30th daye of December 1632.

Wth the Church bookes.

first the chalice with the cover.

A pewtyer flaggine.

A cerples and table clothe.

A carpitte.

A cushine for ye pulpitte and a coveringe Clothe.

One table wth a forme and a Buffett stoole.

vj cowffers (coffers) and vij keys twoe cowffers filled with leade.

vj formes and moulde fraeme for castinge of leade:

A moulde frame.

5 Tressells of wood.

xviij deeds in a boxe xij of yem sealed and vj w'hout seales.

Church books (as before, with the addittion of),

One book of Homilies.

A praire booke of thankesgivinge after ye con-spiracie.

A boke of Cannons (Canons).

Register boke.

Dod and Cleaver.

Codgers househould Government.

Third part of newe watch.

1633	It given unto a Irishman and womane they having a pass to Northumber-land	iijd
	It paide for X yards of Holland to make a newe serples and for makinge of yt	xxvjs vjd

It given to a companie of Irishe foulkes
they havinge a pass allowed by }iiijd
Sr Rich Harpur

1634 It given to one having greatt losses and }xiijd
taken prisoner by Turrkes

It paid to John Cooke for the Communion table and the frame and the }iijli
wealing of it about

1635 It given to a woman that had two
- children iijd

CHAPTER VI.

REPTON'S MERRY BELLS.

" Barrow's big boulders, Repton's merry bells,
Foremark's cracked pancheons, and Newton's egg shells."

THUS does a local poet compare Repton bells
with those of neighbouring parishes. It is not
intended to defend the comparison, for as Dogberry
says, " Comparisons are odorous " ! but to write an
account of the bells, derived from all sources, ancient
and modern.

Llewellynn Jewitt, in Vol. XIII. of the *Reliquary*,
describing the bells of Repton, writes, " at the church
in the time of Edward VI. there were iij great bells & ij
small." Unfortunately " the Churchwardens' and Constables' accounts of the Parish of Repton " only extend
from the year 1582 to 1635. I have copied out most
of the references to our bells entered in them, which
will, I hope, be interesting to my readers.

Extracts from " the Churchwardens' and Constables'
accounts of the Parish of Repton."

A.D. 1583. The levy for the bell   vj^{li} ix^s o
It' spent at takying downe the
     bell   xvj^d
It' payd to the Bellfounder   xxxiij^s iij^d
It' bestowed on the s'vants at
     casting of ye bell   xvj^d

	It' expensys at drawing up the bell	vij[d]
	It' to the ryngers the xvii[th] day of november	xij[d]
A.D. 1584.	Recevyd of the levy for the bell	vj[li] x[s] vij[d]
	It' of Bretby towards the bell	vj[s] viij[d]
	It' spent at taking downe ye bell	viij[d]
	It' bestowed on the bell founder	ij[d]
	It' Payd to Bellfounder for weight, *i.e.*, iiij score & ij pounds	iij[li] xi[s] viij[d]
A.D. 1585.	It' for a bell rope for the great bell	ij[s]
	It' to John Pratt for makinge iiij newe bellropes	v[s]
	It' the day before Saynt Hew's day for mendyng the bels, & for nayles	viij[d]
A.D. 1586	It' of our ladie's even, given to the ringers for the preservation of our Queene	xij[d]
	Our ladie's even, eve of the Annunciation of the Blessed Virgin Mary (March 25th).	
	Preservation of our Queene Elizabeth from the Babington Conspiracy.	
A.D. 1587.	It' given unto the ringers uppon coronation daye	iij[d]
A.D. 1589.	It' for a bell rope	ij[s] viij[d]
A.D. 1590.	It' payde to francis Eaton for mendynge the irons aboutt the bells	ij[s] iiij[d]
A.D. 1592.	It' payde to Ralphe Weanwryghte for trussynge the bells agyne the Coronacyon daye	iij[s]

A.D. 1600.	It' spent in takinge downe ye beell	xij^d
	It' payd to John Welsh for takinge hitt donne	vj^d
	It' spent in lodinge hitt	iiij^d
	It' spent in charges going with the beell to Nottingham, being towe days and one night	vj^s viij^d
	It' payd to ye bellfounder for castinge ye beell	iiij^{li} xviij^s
	It' spent with him	ij^d
	It' payd for yookeinge ye Beell and for greysse	ij^s viij^d
	It' spent uppon them that holpe with the beell	x^d
A.D. 1603.	It' given to the ringers uppon New yeares daye morninge	vj^d
	It' given to ye ringers upon St. James daye (July 25th)	xij^d
	It' given to ye ringers the v daye of August	xij^d
A D. 1605.	It' payd at hanginge up ye greatte bell	vj^d
	It' bestowed of ye Ringers at ye first Ringinge of ye bells	vij^d
	It' payd for greese for ye bells	viij^d
A.D. 1607.	It' given to ye Ringers uppon Christmas daye morning	iiij^d
A D. 1614.	It' towe bellclappers	
A.D. 1615.	The names of them that gave money to bye the newe beell 80 (Repton, 62. Milton, 18.)	
	Sum gathered	xij^{li} viij^s viij^d
A.D. 1623.	First paide for castinge the bell	v^{li}
	It' given to the Ringers at the time of Prince Charlles his comminge forth of spaine. (Oct. 1623).	xij^d

Extract from the diary of Mr. George Gilbert.

" A.D. 1772, Oct. 7th. The third bell was cracked, upon ringing at Mr. John Thorpe's wedding. The bell upon being taken down, weighed 7 cwt. 2 qr. 18lb., clapper, 24lb. It was sold at 10d. per lb., £35. 18s. Re-hung the third bell, Nov. 21st, 1774. Weight 8 cwt. 3 qr. 24lb., at 13d. per lb., £54. 7s. 8d., clapper, 1 qr. 22 lb., at 22d., £1. 2s. 10d. £55. 9s. 6½d.

This is all the information I can gather about " Repton's merry bells " from ancient sources.

For some time our ring of six bells had only been " *chimed*," as, owing to the state of the beams which supported them, it was considered dangerous to " *ring* " them.

During the month of January, 1896, Messrs. John Taylor and Co., of Loughborough, (descendants of a long line of bell-founders), lowered the bells down, and conveyed them to Loughborough, where they were thoroughly cleansed and examined. Four of them were sound, but two, the 5th and 6th, were found to be cracked, the 6th (the Tenor bell) worse than the 5th. The crack started in both bells from the " crown staple," from which the " clapper " hangs; it (the staple) is made of iron and cast into the crown of the bell. This has been the cause of many cracked bells. The two metals, bell-metal and iron, not yielding equally, one has to give way, and this is generally the bell metal. The " Canons," as the projecting pieces of metal forming the handle, and cast with the bell, are called, and by which they are fastened to the " headstocks," or axle tree, were found to be much worn with age. All the " Canons " have been removed, holes have been drilled through the crown, the staples removed, and new ones have been made which pass through the centre hole, and upwards through a square hole in the headstocks, made of iron, to replace the old wooden ones. New bell-frames of iron, made in the shape of the letter **H**. fixed into oak beams above and below, support the bells, which are now raised about three feet above the bell chamber floor, and thus they can be examined more easily.

During the restoration of the Church in 1886, the opening of the west arch necessitated the removal of the ringers' chamber floor, which had been made, at some period or other, between the ground floor and the groined roof, so the ringers had to mount above the groined ceiling when they had to ring or chime the bells. There, owing to want of distance between them and the bells, the labour and inconvenience of ringing was doubled, the want of sufficient leverage was much felt : now the ringers stand on the ground floor, and with new ropes and new "sally-guides" their labour is lessened, and the ringing improved.

When the bells were brought back from Loughboro' I made careful "rubbings" of the inscriptions, legends, bell-marks, &c., before they were raised and fixed in the belfry. The information thus obtained, together with that in Vol. XIII. of the *Reliquary*, has enabled me to publish the following details about the bells.

The "rubbings" and "squeezes" for the article in the *Reliquary* were obtained by W. M. Conway (now Sir Martin Conway) when he was a boy at Repton School.

The 1st (treble) Bell.

On the haunch, between three lines, one above, two below,

FRAVNCIS THACKER OF LINCOLNS INN ESQ.ᴿ 1721.

a border: fleurs-de-lis (fig. 7) : Bell-mark of Abraham Rudhall, (a famous bell-founder of Gloucester) : border (fig. 7).

A catalogue of Rings of Bells cast by A. R. and others, from 1684—1830, is in the Bodleian Library, Oxford : this bell is mentioned as the gift of Francis Thacker.

Fig. 1.

Fig. 2.

Fig. 3.

Fig. 4.

Fig. 5.

Fig. 6.

Fig 7

Fig. 8.

Fig. 9.

F.C.H.

At the east end of the north aisle of our Church there is a mural monument to his memory.

The 2nd Bell.

On the crown a border of fleurs-de-lis (fig. 9). Round the haunch,

𝔍 𝔰𝔴𝔢𝔢𝔱𝔩𝔶 𝔱𝔬𝔩𝔦𝔫𝔤 𝔪𝔢𝔫 𝔡𝔬 𝔠𝔞𝔩𝔩 𝔱𝔬 𝔱𝔞𝔨𝔢 𝔬𝔫 𝔪𝔢𝔞𝔱𝔩 𝔱𝔥𝔞𝔱 𝔣𝔢𝔢𝔡 𝔱𝔥𝔢 𝔰𝔬𝔲𝔩𝔢

between two lines above and below, then below the same border (fig. 9) inverted.

1622 Godfrey Thacker Iane Thacker

This bell is referred to in the Churchwardens' accounts under dates 1615 and 1623.

The 3rd Bell.

Round the haunch, between two lines,

THO^s GILBERT & IOHN TETLEY
CHVRCHWARDENS 1774
PACK & CHAPMAN OF LONDON
FECIT

Below, a border. semicircles intertwined.

This is the bell referred to in the extract quoted above from George Gilbert's diary.

The 4th Bell.

Round the haunch, between six lines (3 above and 3 below),

✠ 𝔐𝔢𝔩𝔬𝔡𝔦𝔢 𝔑𝔬𝔪𝔢𝔫 𝔊𝔢𝔯𝔢𝔱 𝔐𝔞𝔤𝔡𝔢𝔩𝔢𝔫𝔢

a shield: three bells (two and one), with a crown between them (fig. 1), (Bell mark of Richard Brasyer, a celebrated

Norwich Bell founder, who died in 1513) a lion's head on a square (fig. 2): a crown on a square (fig. 3); and a cross (fig. 5).

The 5th Bell.

Round the haunch, between two lines, one above, one below,

✠ 𝕮𝖔𝖝 𝖉𝖚𝖎 𝖎𝖍𝖚 𝖊𝖕𝖎 𝖛𝖔𝖝 𝖊𝖝𝖚𝖑𝖋𝖆𝖈𝖎𝖔𝖓𝖎𝖘

same marks (except the crown) as No. 4 Bell: a king's head crowned (fig. 4): and a cross (fig. 6). Below this, round the haunch, a beautiful border composed of a bunch of grapes and a vine leaf (fig. 8), alternately arranged.

Below, the Bell mark of John Taylor and Co. within a double circle, a triangle interlaced with a trefoil, and a bell in the centre. Above the circle the sacred emblem of S. John Baptist, the lamb, cross, and flag. The name of the firm within the circle.

RECAST 1896.

The 6th Bell (the tenor Bell).

Round the haunch, between four lines, two above, and two below,

𝕳𝖊𝖈 𝕮𝖆𝖒𝖕𝖆𝖓𝖆 𝕾𝖆𝖈𝖗𝖆 𝕱𝖎𝖆𝖙 𝕿𝖗𝖎𝖚𝖎𝖙𝖆𝖙𝖊 𝕭𝖊𝖆𝖙𝖆
𝕲𝕴𝕷𝕭 𝕾𝕭𝕬𝕼𝕶𝕬𝕽 𝕰𝕾𝕼   𝕷𝖖 𝖆𝖓 𝖂𝕬𝕽𝕯𝕰𝕽𝕾 1677

(no bell marks).

Below, a border like that on the fifth Bell.

RECAST 1896.

G. WOODYATT, VICAR.

J ASTLE,
T. E. AUDEN, } CHURCHWARDENS.

Bell mark of J. Taylor and Co. on the opposite side.

———

(Owing to the difference of the type of the inscription, and names, it is supposed that this bell was recast in 1677, so it may have been one of the "three great bells" in Edward VI.'s time.)

The following particulars of the bells have been supplied by Messrs. John Taylor & Co.

		Diameter.		Height.		Note.	Weight.		
		ft.	in.	ft.	in.		cwt.	qr.	lbs.
No.	I.	2	9½	2	3	C♯	7	3	19
„	II.	2	10¾	2	4⅓	B	7	2	27
„	III.	3	0½	2	4½	A	8	1	18
„	IV.	3	2	2	6½	G♯	9	2	21
„	V.	3	6	2	10	F♯	12	2	26
„	VI.	3	11	3	1	E	17	3	0

Total　　3 tons 4 cwts. 0 qrs. 27 lbs.

Key-note E major.

To complete the octave, two more bells are required, D♯ and E, then indeed Repton will have a " ring " second to none.

CHAPTER VII.

THE PRIORY.

THE PRIORY FOUNDED, &c.

BEFORE we write an account of the next most important event in the history of Repton, viz., the founding of Repton Priory, we must go back to the year 1059, when Calke Abbey is supposed to have been founded by Algar, Earl of Mercia. Dr. Cox is of opinion that it was founded later, at the end of the reign of William (Rufus), or at the beginning of that of Henry I. circa 1100. About that date a Priory of Canons regular of St. Augustine, dedicated to St. Giles, was founded. Many benefactors made grants of churches, lands, &c., a list of all these will be found in Cox's Derbyshire Churches, vol iii., p. 346. There is a curious old Chronicle, written in Latin, by one T(h)omas de Musca, Canon of Dale Abbey. Each section of the Chronicle begins with a letter which, together, form the Author's name, a monkish custom not uncommon. The section beginning with an E. (Eo tempore) records the arrival, at Deepdale, of the Black Canons, as they were called, from Kalc (Calke). Serlo de Grendon, Lord of Badeley or Bradeley, near Ashbourne, "called together the Canons of Kalc, and gave them the place of Deepdale." Here, about 1160, the Canons "built for themselves a church, a costly labour, and other offices," which became known as Dale Abbey, in which they lived for a time, "apart from the social intercourse of men,"

but " they began too remissly to hold themselves in the
service of God ; they began to frequent the forest more
than the church ; more to hunting than to prayer or
meditation, so the King ordered them to return to the
place whence they came," viz., Calke.   During the reign
of Henry II., Matilda, widow of Randulf, 4th Earl of
Chester, who died 1153, granted to God, St. Mary, the
Holy Trinity, and to the Canons of Calke, the working
of a quarry at Repton, (Repton Rocks), together with
the advowson of the church of St. Wystan at Repton,
&c., &c., on condition that as soon as a suitable opportunity should occur, the Canons of Calke should remove
to Repton, which was to be their chief house, and Calke
Abbey was to become subject to it.   " A suitable oppor-
tnnity occurred " during the episcopate of Walter
Durdent, Bishop of Coventry only, at first, afterwards
of Lichfield.   He died at Rome, Dec. 7th, 1159.   The
usual date given for *the founding* of Repton Priory is A.D.
1172, but this must be wrong for the simple reason that
Matilda addresses the Charter of Foundation to Bishop
Walter Durdent, who died, as we saw, in 1159: moreover,
the " remains " of the Priory belong to an earlier date ;
probably the date 1172 refers to the *coming* of the Canons
from Calke to Repton, as Dugdale writes, " About the
year 1172, Maud, widow of Randulf, *removed* the greater
part of them here (Repton), having prepared a church
and conventual buildings for their reception."   To those
interested in Charters, copies of the original, and many
others, can be read in Bigsby's " History of Repton,"
Dugdale's " Monasticon," and Stebbing-Shaw's Article
in Vol. II. of " the Topographer," in which he has copied
several " original Charters, not printed in the Monasticon," which were in the possession of Sir Robert Burdett,
Bart., of Foremark, and others.

The Charters, containing grants, extend from Stephen's
reign, (1135-1154), to the reign of Henry V., (1413-1422),
and include the church of St. Wystan, Repton, with its
chapels of Newton Solney, Bretby, Milton, Foremark,
Ingleby, Tickenhall, Smisby, and Measham, the church

at Badow, in Essex, estates at Willington, including its
church, and Croxall.

In 1278 a dispute arose between the Prior of Repton
and the inhabitants of the Chapelry of Measham, which
had been granted to the Priory about 1271.   The
chancel of Measham Church was " out of repair," and
the question was, who should repair it ?   After considerable debate, it was settled that the inhabitants
would re-build the chancel provided that the Priory
should find a priest to officiate in the church, and
should keep the chancel in repair for ever after, both of
which they did till the dissolution of the Priory.

In the year 1364 Robert de Stretton, Bishop of
Lichfield (1360—1386), was holding a visitation at
Repton in the Chapter House of the Priory.   For some
reason or other, not known, the villagers, armed with
bows and arrows, swords and cudgels, with much
tumult, made an assault on the Priory gate-house.
The Bishop sent for Sir Alured de Solney, and Sir
Robert Francis, Lords of the Manors of Newton Solney
and Foremark, who came, and quickly quelled this
early " town and gown " row, without any actual
breach of the peace.   The monument in the crypt of
Repton Church, where it was placed during the
" restoration " of 1792, is supposed to be an effigy of
Sir Robert Frances.   " The Bishop proceeded on his
journey, and, on reaching Alfreton, issued a sentence
of interdict on the town and Parish Church of Repton,
with a command to the clergy, in the neighbouring
churches, to publish the same under pain of greater
excommunication."   See *Lichfield Diocesan Registers.*

On October 26th, 1503, during the reign of Henry
VII., an inquisition was held at Newark.   A complaint
was heard against the Prior of Repton for not providing
a priest " to sing " the service in a chapel on Swarkeston
Bridge, " nor had one been provided for the space of
twenty years, although a piece of land between the
bridge and Ingleby, of the annual value of six marks,
had been given to the Prior for that purpose."

The Priory of Repton was dissolved in the year 1538. By the advice of Thomas Cromwell—*malleus monachorum* —the hammer of the monks—Henry VIII. issued a commission of inquiry into the condition, &c., of the monasteries in England. A visitation was made in 1535, the results were laid before the House of Commons, in a report commonly known as the "Black Book." In 1536 an Act was passed for the suppression of all monasteries possessing an income of less than £200. a year. By this Act 376 monasteries were dissolved, and their revenues, £32,000. per annum, were granted to the King, by Divine permission Head of the Church! Repton Priory was among them. In the *Valor Ecclesiasticus* (27 Henry VIII.) the gross annual value of the temporalities and spiritualities is given as £167. 18s. 2½d. In 1535, Dr. Thomas Leigh and Dr. Richard Layton, *visited* Repton and gave the amount as £180. Also they reported, as they were expected, that the Canons were not living up to their vows, &c., &c., and " Thomas Thacker was put in possession of the scite of the seid priory and all the demaynes to yt apperteynying to or sov'aigne lorde the Kynges use the xxvj day of October in the xxx yere of or seid sov'aigne lorde Kyng henry the viijth." There is a very full inventory of the goods and possessions in the Public Record Office, *Augmentation Office Book, 172*. A transcript of this inventory is given by Bigsby in his *History of Repton*, also by W. H. St. John Hope, in *Vol. VI.* of the *Derbyshire Archæological Journal*. From this inventory, and Mr. St. John Hope's articles in the journal, a very good account and description can be given of the Priory as it was at the time of its dissolution.

The dissolved Priory was granted to Thomas Thacker in 1539, he died in 1548, leaving his property to his son Gilbert. He, according to Fuller (*Church History, bk. vi., p. 358*), " being alarmed with the news that Queen Mary

had set up abbeys again (and fearing how large a reach
such a precedent might have), upon a Sunday (belike the
better day, the better deed) called together the carpenters
and masons of that county, and plucked down in one day
(churchwork is a cripple in going up, but rides post in
coming down) a most beautiful church belonging thereto,
saying " he would destroy the nest, for fear the birds
should build therein again "." The destruction took place
in the year 1553. How well he accomplished the work is
proved by the ruins uncovered during the years 1883-4.

This Gilbert died in 1563, as set forth on the mural
tablet in the south aisle of Repton Church, a copy of
which I have made, so that my readers may see what
sort of a person he was who " wrought such a deed of
shame." Gilbert sold the remains of the Priory to the
executors of Sir John Port in 1557, he and his descendants
lived at the Hall till the year 1728, when Mary Thacker,
heiress of the Manor of Repton Priory, left it, and other
estates, to Sir Robert Burdett, of Foremark, Bart. Since
that time the Hall has been occupied by the Headmasters
of Repton School.

REPTON PRIORY DESCRIBED.

The Priory followed the usual plan of monastic
buildings, differing chiefly in having the cloister on the
north of its church, instead of the *south*. This alteration
was necessary owing to the river Trent being on the
north. In choosing a site for monasteries the water
supply was of the first consideration, as everything,
domestic and sanitary, depended on that. The Conventual buildings consisted of Gate-house, Cloister,
with Church on its south side, Refectory or Fratry
on its north. The Chapter House, Calefactorium, with
Dormitory above them, on its east side. Kitchens,
buttery, cellars, with Guest Hall over them, on its
west side. The Infirmary, now Repton Hall, " beside
the still waters " of the Trent, on the north of the
Priory. The Priory precincts, (now the Cricket
ground), were surrounded by the existing wall on the

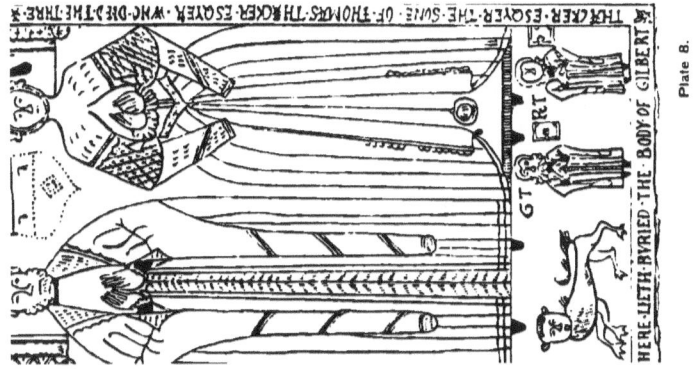

Gilbert Thacker.

(Page 54.)

Plate 8.

west, south, and east sides; on the north flowed, what
is now called, "the Old Trent," and formed a boundary
in that direction.

On the east side of the Priory was the Mill.   The
wall, with arch-way, through which the water made its
way across the grounds in a north-westerly direction, is
still *in situ* in the south-east corner of the Cricket ground.
The Priory, and well-stocked fish ponds, were thus
supplied with water for domestic, sanitary, and other
purposes.

The bed of the stream was diverted to its present
course, outside the eastern boundary wall, by Sir John
Harpur, in the year 1606.

The *Gate-house* (now represented by the School Arch,
which was its outer arch, and wall) consisted of a square
building with an upper chamber, and other rooms on the
ground floor for the use of the porter.   Two "greate
gates," with a wicket door let into one of them, for use
when the gates were closed, or only pedestrians sought
for admission, provided an entrance to the Priory.   Pro-
ceeding through the arch-way of the Gate-house, we find
ourselves in the precincts.   In the distance, on our left
hand, was the Parish Church of St. Wystan, on our
right the Priory Church and conventual buildings.

The *Priory Church* consisted of nave, with north and
south aisles, central tower, north and south transepts,
choir, with aisles, and a south chapel, and a presbytery
'o the east of the choir.   The *Nave* (95 ft. 6 in. long,
and, with aisles, 51 ft. 8 in. wide) " was separated from
the aisles by an arcade of six arches, supported by
clustered pillars of good design, and must have been one
of the most beautiful in this part of the country, all of
exceptionally good character and design, and pertained
to the transitional period of architecture which prevailed
during the reign of Edward I., (1272—1307), when the
severe simplicity of the Early English was merging into
the more flowing lines of the Decorated." In the north
aisle the foundations of an older church, perhaps the
original one, were discovered in 1883-4.

There were several Chapels in the Nave, two of which
are named, viz., "Or lady of petys Chapell" and the
"Chapell of Saint Thomas," with images, "reredoses, of
wood gylte, and alebaster," "and a partition of tymber
seled ouer in seint Thom's Chapell." "vij. peces of tymber
and lytell oulde house of tymber," probably the remains
of a shrine, and "xij. Apostells," *i.e.* images of them.   "j
sacrying bell," sanctus bell, used during the celebration
of the mass.   In the floor, in front of the central tower
arch, a slab was discovered, (6 ft. 4 in. by 3 ft. 2 in.),
bearing a rudely cut cross, with two steps, and an inscription, in Old English letters, partly obliterated, round the
margin "(Orate pro) anima magistri edmundi duttoni
quondam canonici huius ecclisie qui obiit . . . . . januarii
anno diu mccccl° cui' ppic (deus Amen)."   This slab is
now lying among the ruins at the east end of the Pears
School.

Central Tower (25 ft. by 21 ft. 6 in.) supported by four
large piers.   Between the two eastern piers there was a
pulpitum, a solid stone screen (5 ft. 4½ in. deep), with a
door in the centre (4 ft. 4½ in. wide).   In the northern half
was a straight stone stair leading to the organ loft above,
where was "j ould pair of Organs," a phrase often met
with in old inventories, and church accounts, in describing
that instrument of music.   Through the passage under
the screen we enter the *Choir*.   The step leading *down* to
the choir floor, much worn by the feet of the canons and
pilgrims, is still *in situ*.   The Choir (26 ft. wide, 31 ft.
long) was separated from the south Choir aisle, by an
arcade of five arches, from the north choir aisle, by an
arcade of three arches.   All traces of the Canons' stalls
have gone, but there was room for about thirty-four,
thirteen on each side, and four returned at the west end
of the Choir.   In the Choir was the High Altar with
"v. great Images" at the back of which was a retable, or
ledge of alabaster, with little images, on a reredos with
elaborate canopies above them).   "iiij lytle candlestyks"
and "a laumpe of latten," *i.e.*, a metal chiefly composed of
copper, much used in church vessels, also "j rode" or cross.

On the south of the choir was *a chapel dedicated to St. John*, with his image, and alabaster table, similar to that in the choir.   To the south of St. John's Chapel was the "*Chapel our Lady*" similarly ornamented, these two chapels were separated from the south transept by "partitions of tymber," or screens, the holes in which the screens were fixed are still to be seen in the bases of the pillars.   On the east of the choir was the Presbytery.   In the *South Transept* was the Chapel of St. Nicholas with images of St. John and St. Syth, (St. Osyth, daughter of Frithwald, over-lord of the kingdom of Surrey, and Wilterberga daughter of King Penda).   Of the *North Choir Aisle* nothing remains : it is supposed that in it was the shrine of St. Guthlac, whose sanctus bell is thus referred to by the visitors in their report "superstitio—Huc fit peregrinatio ad Sanctum Guthlacum et ad eius campanam quam solent capitibus imponere ad restinguendum dolorem capitis." "Superstition.   Hither a pilgrimage is made to (the shrine of) St. Guthlac and his (sanctus) bell, which they were accustomed to place to their heads for the cure of headache."   The *North Transept* was separated from the north choir aisle by an arcade of three arches, immediately to the east of which the foundations of a wall, about six feet wide, were discovered, which, like those in the north nave aisle, belonged to an older building.   Many beautiful, painted canopies, tabernacle work, &c., were found among the *débris* of the north transept and aisle, which no doubt adorned the shrines, and other similar erections, which, *before* the suppression of the monasteries, had been destroyed, and their relics taken away—that is, probably, the reason why we find no mention of the shrines of St. Guthlac, or St. Wystan in the Inventory.

In the western wall of the North Transept there was a curious recess (13 ft. 10 in. by 4 ft. 10 in., which may have been the *armarium*, or cupboard of *the Vestry*, to hold the various ornaments, and vestments used by the Canons, "j Crosse of Coper, too tynacles, (tunicles), ij albes, ij copes of velvet, j cope of Reysed Velvet, iiij

H

towels & iiij alter clothes, ij payented Alterclothes,"
&c., &c.

Leaving the Church, we enter *the Cloister*, through
the door at the east end of the Nave, it opened into the
south side of the Cloister (97 ft. 9 in. long by 95 ft. wide).
Here were " seats," and "a lavatory of lead," but,
owing to alterations, very little indeed is left except the
outside walls. Passing along the eastern side we come
to the *Chapter House*, the base of its entrance, divided
by a stone mullion into two parts, was discovered,
adjoining it on the north side was a *slype*, or passage,
through which the bodies of the Canons were carried
for interment in the cemetery outside. The *slype*
(11¾ ft. wide by 25½ ft. long) still retains its roof,
"a plain barrel vault without ribs, springing from a
chamfered string course." Next to the slype was the
Calefactorium or warming room. Over the Chapter
House, Slype, and Calefactorium was the *Dormitory*
or *Dorter*, which was composed of cells or cubicles.

The *Fratry* or *Refectory* occupied the north side of
the Cloister, here the Canons met for meals, which
were eaten in silence, excepting the voice of the reader.
A pulpit was generally built on one of the side walls,
from which legends, &c., were read. Underneath the
Fratry was a passage, leading to the Infirmary, and
rooms, used for various purposes, Scriptorium, &c.
At the east end of the Fratry was the *Necessarium*,
well built, well ventilated, and well flushed by the
water from the Mill race.

At the west end of the Fratry was the *Buttery*. The
west side of the Cloister was occupied by the *Prior's
Chamber*, and five others called, in the Inventory,
"*the Inner*," "*Gardyn*," "*Next*," "*Halle*," and "*Hygh
Chambers*." All were furnished with "fether bedds, &c.,
&c.," for the use of guests, who were received and
entertained in this part of the Priory. Underneath these
rooms were "the Kychenn," "Larder," "Bruhouse,"
&c., called the *Cellarium*, over which the Cellarer had
supreme authority. Originally the *Cellarium* was divided

into three parts, Kitchen, Cellar, and Slype or passage
into the south side of the Cloister. The part assigned
to the Kitchen was sub-divided into three rooms, one on
the east side, two on the west. One of these two (the
south) has a vaulted roof, with plain square ribs, the boss
where they meet has been carved, and a part of one
of the ribs has been ornamented with the dog tooth
moulding, for about 18 inches, there it stopped unfinished,
in the walls are many recesses for the reception of
" plate," &c.

The *Cellar* was a long room (89 ft. by 26 ft.), divided
into two "alleys" by a row of six massive Norman
columns, four of which remain, one has a scollopped
capital, the others are plain. The floor above was divided
in a similar manner, with the Prior's Chamber at the
north end, the *Guest Hall*, divided into the various rooms
mentioned above, and a chamber over the slype, which
was probably used as a parlour by the guests.

Besides these there are three houses mentioned, viz.,
" *The Kelyng or Yelyng house*," (Yele-House, *i.e.*, brewing-
house). It' there xvj Kelyngleades and ij mashfattes."

" *The Boultyng house*" (where the meal was bolted or
sifted in the boultyng hutch). It' there ij troffes, j
boultyng huche & j one syve (sieve)."

" *The Kyll-house.*" It' j heyr upon the Kyll & j sestiron
of lead." (Kyll-house = Slaughter house ?)

The contents of all these, including " Grayne " (wheat,
barley, malt, peas, and hay); " Catell " (three " Kye "
cows), ten " horssys," and " two old carts "; and one
Reke (rick) of Peas, sold to Thomas Thacker for the sum
of £40. 2s. 0d., made up of the following items.

	£.	s.	d.
The contents of the Church	2	10	0
,, ,, ,, ,, Vestry	4	0	0
,, ,, ,, ,, Priory	14	19	4
For Grayne and Catell ...	18	12	8
	£40	2	0

This, with the sum of £122. 17s 6d. "Imbesulyd" by John Smyth and Richard haye, made a total of £162. 19s. 6d.

Out of this Rewardes of £2. each were given to the Sub-Prior and eight canons, and sums, varying from 25/s. to 2od., were given to twenty-five servants, and other exs., Total £38. 16s. 6d., so there remained in the hands of the Commissioners £124. 3s. od.

Pensions were also granted to the Sub-Prior and the Canons, varying from £6. to 6s. 8d.

Certain "Whyte Plate" consisting of two Chalices and 10 spoons, Four bells, weighing 24 cwt., and 29 "fothers" of lead remained unsold. A fother was 19½ cwt.

The following is a list of the Priors of Repton, with dates as far as they are known.

Alured, before 1200.
Reginald, about 1230.
Ralph, died 1317.
John de Lych or Lynchfield, 1336.
Simon de Sutton, election confirmed 1st August. (20th Edward III.), 1347.
Ralph de Derby, 1356-7.
William de Tuttebury, 1398.
William Maneysin, 1411.
Wistan Porter, 1420.
John Overton, 1437.
John Wylæ or Wylne, 1439.
Thomas de Sutton, 1471.
Henry Preste, 1486.
William de Derby, 1511.
John Yonge, 1523.
Thomas Rede, sub-prior 1535.
Rauffe Clarke, sub-prior 1538.

Plate 9.

CHAPTER VIII

REPTON SCHOOL.

"THE Foundation of Repton School dates from the middle of that century which is truly described as the age of the revival of learning. It may be that other times have witnessed great changes and progress,—that our own day bears signs of even more wonderful intellectual activity than any that has gone before. But our successes are only the natural results of the achievements of our Fathers,—the gathering in of the Autumn fruits sown in that Spring. The mental revolution of the sixteenth century broke suddenly on the dull cold sleep of past ages, with the mysterious impulse and pregnant energy with which a Scandinavian Spring bursts forth from the bosom of Winter.

"The wisest of our countrymen in those days, men who could at once see before them, and gather wisdom from the past, seem to have discerned the movement when as yet the mass was hardly stirred, and it was their care to provide means to foster and direct it. Kings and Cardinals and Prelates led the way ; Knights and Gentlemen and Yeomen followed. By the munificence of Wolsey and King Henry, the noblest Colleges of Oxford and Cambridge were established :—Edward VI. placed Grammar Schools in all his principal towns ; as Shrewsbury, and Birmingham, and Bath :—and with the same object John Lyon, (yeoman of Harrow), Lawrence Sheriffe, (grocer of London), Sir John Porte,

(Knight of the Bath), founded their schools,"* at Harrow, Rugby and Repton.

The founder of Repton School was descended from a long line of merchants who lived at Chester, then called West Chester, to distinguish it from Manchester.

His father was a student in the Middle Temple, and, after being called to the Bar, filled many offices at it. In the year 1525 he was raised to a Judge-ship of the King's Bench, and was knighted. He married twice, (1) Margery, daughter of Sir Edward Trafford, and (2) Joan, daughter of John Fitzherbert, of Etwall, by whom he had a son, John. After the dissolution of the Monasteries, King Henry VIII. granted to him the Manor, together with the impropriate Rectory and advowson of the Vicarage of Etwall. He is said to have taken some part in the foundation of Brasenose College, Oxford, and, with John Williamson, provided "stipends for two sufficient and able persons to read and teach openly in the hall, the one philosophy, the other humanity."

Of the early days of his son John, nothing is known. He was educated at Brasenose College, where he was the first lecturer or scholar on his father's foundation. At the coronation of King Edward VI. he was made a Knight of the Bath. Like his father, he married twice. His first wife was Elizabeth, daughter of Sir Thomas Giffard, by whom he had two sons, who predeceased him, and three daughters—Elizabeth, who married Sir Thomas Gerard, Knt., of Bryn ; Dorothy, who married George Hastings, Earl of Huntingdon ; and Margaret, who married Sir Thomas Stanhope, Knt., of Shelford. From whom the present hereditary Governors of Repton School, Lord Gerard, Earl Loudoun, and Earl Carnarvon, trace their descent. His second wife was Dorothy, daughter of Sir Anthony Fitzherbert, of Norbury, by whom he had no children. In the year 1553 he was one of the

---

* See Dr. Pears' address at the Tercentenary of Repton School, 1857.

"Knights of the Shire" for the county of Derby, and
served the office of High Sheriff for the same county in
1554. In August, 1556, he "sat with the Bishop of the
diocese (Ralph Baine) and the rest of the Commissioners,
at Uttoxeter, in Staffordshire, to search out heresies
and punish them." (Strype, Memorials, vol. III., part 2,
p. 15.) Joan Waste, a blind woman, was tried and found
guilty of heresy, and was burnt at the stake in Derby.
By will, dated the 6th of June, 1557, among many other
bequests, he gave and devised to his executors, Sir
Thomas Giffard, Richard Harpur, Thomas Brewster,
John Harker, and Simon Starkey, all his lands, tenements and hereditaments, in Mosley, Abraham, and
Brockhurst, in the county of Lancaster, to find a Priest,
well learned and graduate, and of honest and virtuous
conversation, freely to keep a Grammar School in Etwall,
or Repton, also an Usher associate to and with the said
master, to keep the School. The School Master to have
yearly twenty pounds, and the Usher ten pounds.
Also that his executors should hold, for the term of
seven years after his decease, his farm called Musden
Grange, and with the profits should find a priest to
say Mass, &c., for seven years, and with the residue
of the profits of the stock and farm should build a
substantial school-house with convenient chambers and
lodgings for the schoolmaster and usher in the precinct
on the north side of the churchyard of Etwall, or at
Repton, and this being done, without delay, to establish,
by the King and Queen's license, and other assurances
to the School for ever.

He also willed that Sir William Perryn, Bachelor of
Divinity, his late Chaplain, should be (if living and willing)
the first Schoolmaster.

As the Report, made to the Charity Commissioners by
F. O. Martin, Esq., in 1867, says, "Sir John had no
property in Repton. His executors were probably induced
to establish the school there, rather than at Etwall, by
finding the remains of the dissolved priory well adapted
to the purpose."

By a deed, dated June 12th, 1557, "Gilbert Thacker of Repton, in consideration of the sum of £35. 10s., bargained and sold to Richard Harpur, serjeant-at-law, John Harker, and Simon Starkey, three of Sir John Porte's executors, one large great and high house, near the kitchen of Gilbert Thacker, commonly called the Fermery (Infirmary) (now the Hall), also one large void room or parcel of ground upon the east part called the Cloyster, and one other room called the Fratry, (now destroyed), upon which the Schoolmaster's lodgings were erected and builded, with all the rooms, both above and beneath, and inclosed with a new wall, to the intent that the same should be a schoolhouse and so used from time to time thereafter."

Thus was Repton School founded by Sir John Porte. The management seems to have been in the hands of the Harpurs till the year 1621, when an agreement was made by Sir John Harpur on the one part, and Henry, Earl of Huntingdon, Philip, Lord Stanhope, and Sir Thomas Gerard, Bart., on the other, by which, after the death of Sir John Harpur, the management was restored to the rightful descendants of the founder.

In 1622, on the petition of the above-mentioned co-heirs of Sir John, by Royal Letters Patent, bearing date 20th June, 19th Jac., I., a Charter of Incorporation by the style and title of "The Master of Etwall Hospital, the School Master of Repton, Ushers, Poor Men, and Poor Scholars," was granted. "That, owing to the increased value of the lands and tenements, it should consist of one Master of the Hospital, one School Master, two Ushers, twelve Poor Men, and four Poor Scholars, and that Sir John Harpur should be the first and present Governor and Superintendent of the School and Hospital, and that after his death the co-heirs should manage them. The co-heirs "of their friendliness and goodwill to Sir John Harpur" petitioned that his heirs should have the election and appointment of three of the twelve poor men, and one of the poor scholars, which was also granted, and they continue to do so to this day."

CHAPTER IX.

REPTON SCHOOL v. GILBERT THACKER.

LL Reptonians and visitors to Repton know the two pillars, and low wall which divide the School yard into two, almost equal, parts. Bigsby and others believe that the wall is the boundary of the two Manors of Repton.

In the year 1896 I found, in the School muniment chest, among a lot of musty, fusty documents, deeds, &c., two rolled-up folios, lawyers' briefs, with interrogations, depositions, &c. On the back of one of the briefs is a very rough pen and ink sketch-plan of the School buildings, &c. This has served to identify the various portions occupied by the School and the Thackers, described in the last chapter, and also gives the reason why the wall was built. It appears that during the life-time of Godfrey Thacker, grandson of Gilbert, the destroyer of the Priory, the "schollers" of Repton School used to annoy him, while working in his study, by playing too near his house, many rows ensued. These went on till the days of Godfrey's son Gilbert : he determined either to put an end to the annoyances, or to the School, he did not care which, as we shall see.

In 1652, soon after he succeeded to the estates, he commenced a suit against the School. Gilbert Thacker, plaintiff, John Jennings, Master of Etwall Hospital, William Ullock, Headmaster of Repton School, and others, defendants.

1

" Plaintiff declared that the defendants the 1st day of December, 1651, with force and armes the close of the said Gilbert, called the greate or broade court (the School yard) at Repton did breake and enter and his grasse there lately growing to the value of one hundred shillings with their feete walkinge did treade downe and consume to the damage of £40."

Defendants pleaded not guilty, and produced twelve witnesses, O.R.s and others, who proved that " the scholemasters used to walke up and downe the broade court at their pleasures, and the schollers have used to play there . . . . That some scholemasters that kept cowes have used to turne there cowes into the yard. (Mr. Watson stalled them in a room in the Priory itself!) That Thacker's father (Godfrey) was a barrister-at-law, and never questioned it although continually used."

The matter was settled "out of court," by the appointment of two arbitrators, Sir Francis Burdett, Bart., and Sir Samuel Sleigh, Knt., (O R.s), with Gervase Bennett, as referee. They pronounced "theire award by word of mouth about the yeare 1653." Thacker was to build a wall across the Court, beyond which the boys were not allowed to pass. This he refused to do, so the alleged trespass, and annoyances went on for another twelve years, when, owing to the conduct of Gilbert, the School brought an action against him. "The schollers with threats of smites and blows were affrighted, many of them were assaulted and beaten, many to avoyd effusion of blood and expenses have absented themselves for a week together, thro' fear of arrest, some have withdrawn to other schooles. If theire hats blew over the " Causey " (the entrance to the School) they durst not fetch them, if Mr. Thacker was in the way."

He also employed one Godfrey Kinton, a carpenter, to set up "stoopes and rayles (post and rails) from the Chancell nooke to the nooke of the nether School House chimney below the door," but alas! boys were boys even then, for we read when " he set up one stoope, and went for more, before he returned, the stoope was pulled up, and earth thrown into the hole by the schollers !"

Gilbert also tried in a more offensive way to make the occupants of the Schoole House " weary of being there." Down the School yard "uppon a sudden rush of raine there was usually a water-course through the Court-yard into Mr. Thacker's inner court . . . . and soe under the dogg kennell to the river." This course he stopped " with stones and clodds, and caused the water to run into the School House ! twenty-seven or eight pales-full of water had been ladled out." When Mr. Ullock (the Headmaster) complained, and requested that the stones and clods might be taken away, he was bidden "to take them away himself if he durst, this the schollers did more than once."

Mrs. Ullock came in for a share of the "smites and blows." For, we read, "one day Gilbert Thacker furiously assaulted Mrs. Ullock as she stood at her own door, and flung her into the house, followed her and strucke her." His wife joined in the fray, " she strucke Mrs. Ullock, and tore her own gorgett upon a neale." . . . . "Ann Heyne, being by, interceded for her mistress, whereupon Gilbert strucke her and felled her to the grounde, and gave her a foule pinch by the arm, and again strucke Mrs. Ullacke," then Mrs. Thacker and her son "ran up to Mr. Ullock's studdy and told him that his wife had abused *her* husband !" So we are not surprised to hear that the School brought an action against the Thackers. The High Court of Chancery appointed four gentlemen, as Commissioners, to try the case. William Bullock (O.R.), Daniel Watson, Esquires, Thomas Charnells, and Robert Bennett, gentlemen. They met " at the house of Alderman Hugh Newton, at Derby, there being at the signe of the George."

There they summoned witnesses to attend ; fifty did so, twenty-five a side. Their depositions, in answer to interrogatories, were taken on April 15th, 1663, and fill sixty pages of folio. As before mentioned, they consist of two folios, one for the School and one for Thacker. The chief questions administered to the witnesses for the School, referred to their knowledge of the School buildings, Schoolmasters and boys, Thacker's ancestors, rights of way, award of Sir Francis Burdett, and Sir Samuel Sleigh, former suits at law, the Thackers' conduct, the value of the land, as grass land, and the use of the yard for recreation by the boys, &c. For Thacker, the questions asked referred to their knowledge of prohibitions by his ancestors and himself, and complaints made to the Schoolmasters, &c.

The depositions are most interesting, as the knowledge of witnesses extended back to within forty years of the founding of the School.

The number of Schoolmasters varied—in Watson's time two, in Whitehead's three, Schoolmaster, Middle Master, and Usher. The number of boys also varied from 60 to 200, with "7 or 8 poor schollers." Among the boys mentioned were four sons of Philip, first Earl of Chesterfield, Philip, Charles, George and Ferdinando Stanhope ; Michael Folliott, son of Henry Folyot, Foleott or Ffoliott, Baron of Ballyshannon, Ireland ; Wingfield, Thomas, Vere Essex, and Oliver Cromwell, the four sons of Thomas Cromwell, first Earl of Ardglass, besides the sons of divers knights and gentlemen, Sir Francis Burdett, Bart., Sir Samuel Sleigh, Knt., Godfrey Meynell, Thomas Sanders, William Bullock, &c., &c., most of whom had gone to the Universities of Oxford or Cambridge. (See *Repton School Register*)

The " Court yard " (School yard) had been used by the boys to recreate themselves in, without let or hindrance from the defendant's ancestors. The award was well known, and agreed to at the time, 1653, but the defendant had refused to comply with it, and had stopped several ways, and blocked up a door leading to the brook, from the north-east corner of the Schoolmaster's garden.

The evidence of Ann Heyne, &c., referred to above, proved that the defendant s conduct had " caused many brawls, and many schollers to be affrighted and absent themselves from schoole." The value of the land was worth from 2d. to 6d. per annum!

The defendant's witnesses agreed about most of the points in dispute, but they said the boys had no right to play in the great court yard without permission, and some of them remembered having been whipped by Godfrey Thacker and Schoolemaster Watson for so doing, and others remember playing in " the Staineyard," by orders of the Schoolemasters Watson and Whitehead. Defendant also objected to the disposal of ashes, which the Headmaster used to have placed on a mound opposite his front door, and the Usher at the back of the Causey (*i.e.* the way between the stone walls, leading into the old big school) instead of in the garden at the back of the School, as they used to be put, as one witness said " he had seen them carried by Mr. Schoolemaster Watson's daughter!"

The Commissioners " recommended the differences between the two parties to the Right Honourable Philipp, Earl of Chesterfield, to call the said parties before him, and to hear and finally determine the said differences between them if his Worship so can." Gilbert Thacker again failed to carry out the terms agreed upon, so on the 11th day of January, in the 18th year of the reign of Charles II., King, a writ was issued against him for contempt of court. The writ is in the Muniment Chest, and it is a rare specimen of a legal document in Latin, written short, full of abbreviations, very difficult to decipher, as Thacker pleaded in his answer, " it was written in short lattin, some of the words written very short, he did not well understand it, nor could say if it was a true Coppy," when Mr. Motteram (counsel for the School) delivered it to him, and read it over to him, but he was wise enough to understand and obey it eventually, so his contempt was pardoned, and in the following year a final agreement was made between him and the School.

(1) The School to build up the way out of the School

House garden in the north wall, and to give up all
rights to go (that way) to the Brook.

(2) Also to give up the Void piece of ground called the
Slaughter House Yard (now the Hall Garden)
between the School House and Thacker's Kitchen.

(3) A wall was to be built, by both parties, from the
Chancel north-east Corner, to the north side of the
door of the Nether School House.

4) And the boys were allowed to play between the
wall and the Greate Gate (the School Arch).

A receipt for £14. 19s. od., half the cost of building the
wall, signed by Wm. Jordan, proves the wall, and pillars
were built, or finished in May, 1670, and the long continued disputes ceased.

In Dr. Sleath's time the gates were removed, and the
wall, which at first was nearly level with the capitals of
the pillars, was taken down on the west side, and lowered
on the east, as it is now. This is the history of the
pillars and wall, as recorded in the deeds, &c., lately
discovered in the Muniment Chest, which may contain
other interesting details of events long ago forgotten in
the history of Repton School, and may be unearthed
(literally) out of the dust of ages !

CHAPTER X.

REPTON TILE-KILN.

AT various times and places within the precincts of Repton Priory tiles have been dug up. In the year 1851 the British Archæological Association held a Congress at Derby, and a visit was made to Repton. Its members examined, among other interesting things, some remarkably fine specimens of encaustic tiles, which Dr. Peile, then Headmaster, had dug up, on or about the site of the Priory Church, but it was not till the year 1866 that the kiln itself was discovered. This discovery cannot be better described than in the words of Dr. Pears, quoted from *The Reliquary*, January, 1868.

"Through the months of October and November, 1866, the boys of Repton School were busily engaged in levelling a piece of uneven grass land within the Old Abbey (Priory) Wall. During the work they came unexpectedly upon patches of a stiff red clay, quite unlike the ordinary soil of the place, with here and there fragments of encaustic tiles, such as have from time to time been found in other parts of the Old Abbey (Priory) grounds. Presently they found a considerable number of whole tiles of various patterns, in two rows of layers, placed face downwards. On the sixth of November they struck upon brickwork, so covered and choked with the clay and broken tiles that it was extremely difficult to clear it." When the accumulated mass of broken tiles and clay had been cleared away, it proved to be a tile-kiln, "one of the most perfect mediæval kilns hitherto unearthed in England." It consisted of two chambers, side by side, seven feet six inches long, two feet six inches wide, and about one foot ten inches high. Six arches of chamfered bricks or tiles, specially made for the purpose, supported a flat roof. Between the arches were recesses wide enough to receive the tiles placed there to be burnt, hundreds of which were found piled up one upon another, but, as they were unburnt, they were soft and pliable, and soon crumbled away. Among the *débris*, however, many whole tiles and fragments were found, greatly varying in pattern. The more perfect specimens were placed over the fire-place in the old " big school," and formed a most interesting mantel-piece. When the room was dismantled in 1889 they were taken down and placed in a cupboard in the inner room till a suitable place can be found for them.

During the excavations made in 1883—5 on the site of the Priory Church, many more tiles were discovered which, with many carved stones, have been affixed to the old north aisle wall, where they can be seen in various stages of decay, suffering from the effects of exposure to our climate.

Among the tiles discovered in 1866, Mr. Llewellyn Jewitt writes, (*Reliquary, Jan.* 1868), " are examples different in form, as well as in material and design, from any others which had come under my notice, made of light stone-coloured clay, the foliated pattern in very high and bold relief, and covered with a rich green glaze." One consists of the crowned letter M, terminated at either end with a crowned letter A, with foliage, all in high relief, and green glazed. The letters are the initial ones of *Ave Maria*, and probably adorned the " Chapel of Our Lady" in the Priory Church, where one was found during the excavations. Among the *single tile* patterns, of which these two are the most beautiful, are many very curious ones, armorial bearings of England, with label of

France, the de Warrenes, de Burghs, Berkeleys, and
Hastings, &c. Alphabet. Fleur-de-lis. Emblems of
Saints Peter and Paul, (Bell, Key, and Sword).
Grotesques, (men, animals, birds, &c.) One, bearing
the name Redlington and arms, which some suppose
stand for Bridlington, and the arms of the founder
(Gant) of that priory. Geometrical, Foliage, especially
oak leaves, with acorns. Another is divided into nine
square compartments, (stamp used, intended for smaller
tiles,) in the centre a flower, right-hand top corner,
arms of De Warrene, left-hand bottom corner, arms of
Berkeley, the others, a double fleur-de-lis, a cross lozengy
between four pellets, a rabbit, a martlet, and two grotes-
que animals.

Of *four tile* patterns there are some good examples,
geometrical designs with foliage (oak leaves), and
armorial bearings.

There are also some remarkably rich and beautiful
sixteen tile patterns. One has a border of curving foliage
between a double circle, within the circle is a quatre-foil,
enclosing a most elegant foliage design, in the centre is
an octagonal flower, in the cusps formed by the quatre-
foil are figures of hares playing, in the corners of the
tile are two pigeons, facing each other, with a cross, with
double head, issuing from their beaks, like Sir John Port's
crest. A second is similar to this, but the centre is
wanting. A third, also circular, still more elaborate,
with dragons in the corners.

There are also some elegant border tiles, with patterns,
consisting of undulating or waving foliage, or birds
perched on the side of a straight branch, with double
circles and pellets between them.

Besides these there are some curious examples of tiles
simply indented or stamped, with circles and foliage, and
painted within the pattern with green glaze, not filled
with "slip," as the liquid clay was called, and two have
a pattern which has evidently been cut or incised with
some sharp instrument, not stamped as all the rest have
been.

K

The size of the tiles varies from 10 inches square to 2½ inches square, by 1¾ inches to 1 inch thick. The body-clay is red, the patterns are filled in with white or yellow "slip," which is brushed or poured over the face of the tile, then the " slip " is scraped off the surface of the tile, leaving " slip " in the pattern. Glazes of various colours, green, yellow, buff, brown, &c. The stamps were most probably made of wood, and vary in size.

The discovery of the tile-kiln enabled Llewellyn Jewitt to *localise* the manufacture of tiles which he had examined in various churches in Derbyshire, especially at Newton Solney, Thurgaton Priory, and Bakewell. A larger tile-kiln was discovered at Dale Abbey, about thirty-eight years ago, close to the ruins of the gatehouse of that Abbey.

The comparison of the tiles, made there and at Repton, forms another link between them, and proves that, at least, similar stamps were used in the production of the tiles, and it may be, as suggested by Mr. John Ward, F.S.A., (" Mediæval Pavement and Wall Tiles of Derbyshire," Vol. XIV., of the " Derbyshire Archæological Journal,") " that stamps were passed on from tilery to tilery, or that companies of tile-wrights, carrying about with them their stamps, &c., temporarily settled down at places where tileries existed."

Repton School Chapel.

(Page 77.)

Plate 10.

Mr. Exham's House.

CHAPTER XI.

REPTON SCHOOL TERCENTENARY

AND FOUNDING OF THE SCHOOL CHAPEL, &c.

THE year 1857 was a memorable one for Repton School, for three hundred years it had existed with varied progress.

A goodly company of Old Reptonians assembled to commemorate the event on Tuesday the 11th of August. They dined together in the old "big school," the Honourable George Denman presided, and was supported by the Masters of Etwall Hospital, and Repton School, and many others.

The next day a much larger number of invited guests arrived. They again assembled in the "big school." At eleven o'clock the Right Honourable Earl Howe, Chairman of the Governors of Etwall Hospital and Repton School arrived, the head boy, W. L. Mugliston, delivered a Latin speech. The Headmaster, Dr. Pears, read an account of the Founder, and founding of the Hospital and School, of its incorporation by royal charter, granted by King James I. in 1622, and subsequent benefactions to the School. He, further, gave an address on the principles, objects, and practical working of the School, and other kindred institutions. After this all proceeded to the Church, where they were received by the Incumbent of Repton, the Rev. W. Williams. The prayers were read by him, and the Headmaster, the lessons by the Rev. G. M. Messiter,

and the Rev. G. P. Clarke. The sermon was preached
by Dr. Vaughan, the Headmaster of Harrow, the text
chosen was Romans xi. 36, "For of Him, and through
Him, and to Him, are all things : to whom be glory
for ever. Amen."

After the service the visitors, &c., had luncheon in
the "big school," a few speeches were made, and the
Rev. T. Woodrooffe, Canon of Winchester, a parent,
suggested that a lasting memorial of that day should be a
School Chapel, a most liberal response was made to the
appeal.

Hitherto the School had worshipped in the Church,
but increasing numbers had made "the building of a
school chapel," as Dr. Pears said, "no longer a matter
of choice, but of necessity." A site within the arch was
applied for, but without success : at last the present site
was procured, and on August 26th, 1858, in the presence
of a large number of visitors, the foundation stone was
laid. After a special service, Dr. Pears presented a
silver trowel to Earl Howe, who, striking the stone
twice with a mahogany mallet, said, "In the name of
the Father, Son, and Holy Ghost, I declare this stone
duly laid."

Underneath the stone a bottle was placed containing
various coins of the realm, and a parchment, bearing the
following memoranda :—

Stet Fortuna Domus.
REPTON SCHOOL CHAPEL.
In commemoration of the 300th Anniversary of the Foundation of
SIR JOHN PORT'S SCHOOL AND HOSPITAL.
The first stone was laid August 26th, 1858,
By RICHARD WILLIAM PENN EARL HOWE,
Acting Governor of the School and Hospital.
Hereditary Governors of the School and Hospital :
EARL HOWE, for Marquis of Hastings, a minor ;
EARL CHESTERFIELD ; SIR R. GERARD, Bart.
Master of the Hospital—REV. W. E. MOUSLEY ;
Headmaster of the School—S. A. PEARS, D.D. ;
First Usher—REV. G. M. MESSITER.
Second Usher—REV. G. P. CLARKE.

BUILDING COMMITTEE.

Hon. G. Denman.

Dr. Pears.

Rev. W. E. Mousley.

Rev. G. M. Messiter.

Rev. G. P. Clarke.

A. Hewgill, Esq., M.D.

T. P. Bainbrigge, Esq.

A. N. Mosley, Esq.

I. Clay, Esq.

B. W. Spilsbury, Esq.

Rev. J. F. Bateman.

Rev. E. J. Selwyn.

Rev. J. Davies.

C. Worthington, Esq.

Architect—I. H. STEVENS.   Builders—Messrs. LILLEY & ELLIOTT.

SCHOOL CHAPEL.

The Chapel originally consisted of nave and two transepts, with a five-light window in the east end. In 1867 a semi-octagonal apse was added at the east end, in memory of Mrs. Pears, who died in April, 1866. In 1880 the nave was extended, two bays, westwards, and an organ, built by Messrs. Gray and Davidson, was fixed to its west wall. In 1884-5 a south aisle was added, the organ removed to its east end, the middle window inserted in the west wall of the nave, and gas was introduced. The style of the building is Perpendicular.

To the memory of Masters, Boys, &c., many of the windows in the apse, south transept, south aisle, and nave, have been filled with stained glass, most of them by Messrs. J. Powell and Sons, of Whitefriars, London.

The windows in the apse, three pairs of lights, are full-length figures of Moses and John the Baptist, two of Our Lord, and S.S. Peter and Paul. Beneath the figures are medallions illustrating an event in their lives; (1) Moses striking the rock, (2) John baptizing our Lord, (3) Jesus in the home at Nazareth, (4) Jesus with S.S. Peter, James and John, (5) S.S. Peter and John at "the gate Beautiful," (6) S. Paul preaching at Athens.

IN MEMORIAM HENRICI ROBERTI HUCKIN HANC FENE-
STRAM AMICI POSUERUNT.

In the south transept, a beautiful little window, our Lord with an infant in His lap.

TO THE GLORY OF GOD, AND IN LOVING MEMORY OF E.S.F. 30TH SEP. 1887.

In the south aisle are six pairs of lights, with full-length figures and medallions, illustrating the Beatitudes.

(1)   " Blessed are the meek." (Moses and S. Timothy.)

PLACED BY MANY SCHOOL AND COLLEGE FRIENDS IN MEMORY OF R. S. MURRAY SMITH, WHO DIED AT ORIEL COLLEGE OXFORD 17TH NOV. 1886. AGED 21.

(2)   "Blessed are the pure in heart." (Daniel and S. John.)

IN MEMORY OF EDWARD PREST, M.A., MASTER AT THIS SCHOOL FROM 1880-87. DIED OCT. 18, 1893.

(3) " Blessed are they that hunger and thirst after righteousness." (David and S. Paul.)

EUSTACE MACLEOD FORBES. BORN NOV. 21, 1862. DIED FEB. 11, 1894.

(4)   " Blessed are the merciful." (Joseph and S. Barnabas.)

FRANCIS HAMAR ELLIOT. BORN AP. 19, 1875. DIED SEP. 6, 1894.

(5) " Blessed are they which are persecuted." (Abel and S. Stephen.)

IN LOVING MEMORY OF EUSTACE GEORGE DAVID MAXWELL, WHO DIED DEC. 22, 1884. AGED 18.

(6)   " Blessed are the peacemakers." (Abraham and S. James.)

IN THANKFUL MEMORY OF HENRY HUGHES DOBINSON, ARCHDEACON OF THE NIGER, WHO AFTER SERVING GOD AS A BOY AT THIS SCHOOL DIED IN HIS MASTER'S SERVICE AT ASABA. AP. 13TH, 1897. AGED 33 YEARS.

At the west end of the south aisle is a three-light
window. Subject : " Christ the Light of the World."

IN DEI GLORIAM EX AMORE HUJUS SACELLI JOSEPHUS
ET JOHANNES GOULD HANC FENESTRAM INSERENDAM
CURAVERUNT A.S. MDCCCLXXXV.

The rose window in the west end of the nave was
placed there by E. Estridge, Esq., in 1881.

The three lights below representing Faith, Hope,
and Charity.

(1) IN DEI GLORIAM UNUS E MAGISTRIS.   (2) IN MEMORIAM
JOHANNIS DOUGLAS BINNEY HUJUS SCHOLÆ E MAGISTRIS
OB. ID. JUN. MDCCCLXXXIII.   (3) IN DEI GLORIAM
REPANDUNENSES.

At the east end of the nave is a beautiful window with
angels and flowers.

" IN THE BLESSED HOPE OF EVERLASTING LIFE WE
DEDICATE THIS WINDOW TO THE MEMORY OF OUR
DEARLY LOVED SON FREDERICK WILLIAM HESSE WHO
FELL ASLEEP AT REPTON MAR. 16, 1895. AGED 14 YEARS.
A. AND M. H."

On the walls in the apse are three brasses in memory
of three Headmasters—Drs. Peile, Pears and Huckin.
In the choir are brasses in memory of Mr. Messiter,
Mr. Johnson and Mr. Latham, Assistant Masters.

In the south transept a brass in memory of the
Right Honble. George Denman.

Mrs. Huckin presented the brass lectern to the Chapel
in 1880.

In 1884 a bell, bearing the following inscription,

DEO D.D. TRES ARCHIDIDASCALI FILIOLÆ,

was placed in the chapel turret.

On the nave walls are brasses in memory of the
following boys :—C. P. Aylmer, J. H. P. Lighton,
J. A. Barber, C. F. Blagg, N. Baskerville Mynors,
H. Goodwin Brooks, F. Levy, A. S. Darrock, J. Strat-
ford Collins.

On the outside of the Chapel, round the three sides of the apse, and along the south side, are the following inscriptions :—

AD MAJOREM DEI GLORIAM ET E. T. P. DESIDERATISSIMÆ
IN MEMORIAM A.S. MDCCCLXVII.

DEO SERVATORI HANC ÆDEM SCHOLÆ REPANDUNENSIS
PER ANNOS CCC INCOLUMIS PRÆSIDES ALUMNI AMICI
POSUERUNT A.S. MDCCCLVIII. AUGENDAM. CURAVERUNT
A.S. MDCCCLXXX.

Repton Hall, from the North.

(Page 81.)

Plate 11.

Porter's Lodge.

(Page 86.)

CHAPTER XII.

SCHOOL HOUSES, &c.

FOR over two hundred years Repton School was held in the Priory, the " School Master " lodged at its north end, and the " Usher " at its south.   Between "the lodgings " was the school-room, known to many generations of Reptonians as the " big school."   A smaller room was built on to this, with a door of communication between them, this room used to be divided into two, the upper end was the Headmaster's study, and the lower end the School library.

During the eighteenth century a large number of boys, who came from a distance, used " to table," that is lodge, in the village.

On January 8th, of the year 1728, Mary Thacker died, leaving Repton Hall to Sir Robert Burdett, Bart., of Foremark.   It is supposed that the School acquired the Hall, as a residence for the Headmaster, about this time.

Repton Hall, originally an isolated brick tower, two storeys high, with hexagonal turrets in the upper storey, was built by Prior Overton during the reign of Henry VIth (1422—1461), and was called Prior Overton's Lodge, but as the Prior, according to the Statutes, was obliged to reside in the Priory itself, moreover the Prior's chamber is named in the Inventory (p. 58), " there can be little doubt," as Mr. St John Hope writes (*Vol. VI., Derbyshire Archæological Journal, p.* 96), " the building was really the infirmitorium, or abode of sick and infirm monks." Like all the other ancient buildings in Repton, additions and

L

restorations have quite changed it. The Thackers added to it when they obtained possession in 1539, and built its southern side during the reign of William and Mary. The only unaltered part is the brick tower, except its top which used to be castellated. (see picture in Bigsby's Hist , Plate 1.)

The lower storey of it, now the kitchen, has a fine oak ceiling divided into nine square compartments by oak beams, at the intersections there are four carved bosses bearing (1) a name device, or rebus of Prior Overton a tun or cask, encircled by the letter **O**, formed by a vine branch with leaves and grapes, (2) a capital **T** ornamented with leaves, (3) an **S** similarly ornamented, (4) a sheep encircled like No. 1. The letters **T** and **S** are supposed to be the initials of former priors.

" The lofty staircase of majestic oak, dim-lighted by an ancient window, filled with narrow panes of deep-discoloured glass," is now brightened with a stained glass window, which was presented and placed in the School Library by Dr. Sleath on his retirement from the headmastership in 1830. It contains armorial bearings of the Founder, and three Hereditary Governors of Repton School, the Earls of Huntingdon, and Chester-field, and Sir John Gerard.

The window was removed to the Hall by Dr. Peile, with Dr. Sleath's knowledge.

Dr. Prior, Headmaster from 1767-79, raised the number of boys to over two hundred, and it is generally thought that he was the first to occupy the Hall. The School Register was so badly kept, or not kept at all, it is difficult to say how many there were with any certainty. When Dr. Pears was appointed in 1854 there were only forty-eight boys in the School, in three years the number was one hundred and eight, and soon it became necessary to build more houses, the difficulty was to obtain sites. The Tercentenary of Repton School, 1857, proved to be a fresh starting point in its history. A site for the School Chapel was applied for within the Arch, but in vain, at last the

Plate 12.

Pears Memorial Hall Window.

(Page 83.)

XII.   SCHOOL HOUSES, ETC.   83

piece of land on which it stands, was obtained with a
further piece at the back of it, on this Dr. Pears built a
house for Mr. Johnson, who opened it in the year 1860.

The Rev. E. Latham opened his house about the
same time. It had formerly been a malt house and
cottages.

Dr. Pears bought the " Old Mitre Inn " and converted
it into a house for the Rev. Joseph Gould in 1865.

In 1869 a house, built by Mr. Estridge, was opened.

In 1871, the Rev. G. P. Clarke (now Clucas) moved
from the south end of the Priory, and opened the house
in which he now lives, in 1883 he resigned his master-
ship, and his boys were transferred to other houses.

In 1880, another Inn ("New Mitre") was converted
into a house, and occupied by the Rev. A. F. E. Forman.

In 1885, Mr. Gurney built his house.

The Pears Memorial Hall, and rooms beneath it, built
on the site of the Priory Chapel, were opened on Speech
Day, June 17th, 1886. The Hall is one hundred and one
feet long, by forty-three feet wide, with a fine open roof,
forty feet high, supported by wall pieces, with hammer
beams, which rest on corbels of stone, carved to represent
shields. The walls are lined with oak panelling, seven
feet high, on them the names of O.R s who have gained
honours at the Universities are being painted. At the
west end there is a magnificent three-manual organ, by
Brindley and Foster of Sheffield, on either side and in
front are raised seats and platform, which form an
orchestra capable of seating one hundred and twenty
performers. At the east end is a large window of fifteen
lights, five in a row, filled with stained glass by Messrs.
James Powell and Sons, of Whitefriars, London. The
lights of the window illustrate the history of Repton from
earliest times. Beginning with the top five (1) St Chad,
bishop of Mercia, founder of the See of Lichfield, A.D. 669.
(2) St. Guthlac, once an inmate of Repton Abbey. (3)
Matilda, Countess of Chester, foundress of Repton Priory,
circa 1150. (4) St. Wereburga, (daughter of King
Wulphere), said to be the first Abbess of Repton. (5)

St. Wystan, (murdered by his cousin Berfurt at Wistanstowe, A.D. 850), buried at Repton, patron saint of its
church.

The middle five contain armorial bearings of (1) The See
of Lichfield. (2) Philip and Mary, in whose reign the
School was founded. (3) Sir John Porte, the founder of
the School. (4) James I., who granted a Charter to
the School. (5) The See of Southwell.

The bottom five full-length figures of (1) Sir Thomas
Gerard. (2) George Hastings, Earl of Huntingdon.
(3) Sir John Porte. (4) Sir Thomas Stanhope. (5) Sir
Richard Harpur. 1, 2, and 4 married Sir John Porte's
three daughters, and are now represented by Lord Gerard,
Earl of Loudoun, Earl of Carnarvon, 5, one of his
executors, ancestor of Sir Vauncey Harpur-Crewe, these
four are Hereditary Governors of Repton School and
Etwall Hospital.

Under the window, on a brass tablet, is the following
inscription :—

HANC   FENESTRAM
REPANDUNENSIBUS   REPANDUNENSIS
JOHANNES   GOULD.   A.M.
A.   S.   MDCCCXCIV.
DONO   DEDIT.

The principal entrance to the Hall is up a staircase
in the tower at the east end, there is also an entrance at
the west end.

Beneath the Hall are four Class-rooms, a " Common-
room " for the Masters, and lavatories. The rooms open
into a Cloister which is on the south side of the building.
The Governing Body of Repton School paid for the
rooms below out of the School funds, the Hall itself being
paid for by friends, old pupils, &c., of Dr. Pears. The
architect was Sir Arthur Blomfield, A.R.A., and the
style, Perpendicular. On June 17th, 1886, The Honble.
Mr. Justice Denman, (O.R.,) presided at the opening, and
declared the Hall opened in these words, " I declare this
Schoolroom, which has been built in the faith of Jesus
Christ, and in memory of His servant, Steuart Adolphus

Mr. Cattley's and Mr. Forman's Houses

Plate 13.

Mr. Gould's House.

Pears, to be now open." Then, after a few dedicatory prayers, and the singing of the "Old Hundredth," speeches were delivered by Mr. Denman, Rev. W. Johnson, (the Senior Assistant Master), Mr. Etherington-Smith, and the Rev. J. H. Clay, O.R s, and the Headmaster (the Rev. W. M Furneaux).

Over the door at the east end is a brass tablet bearing the following inscription :—

IN HONOREM PRÆCEPTORIS OPTIMI

STEUART ADOLPHI PEARS S.T.P.

SCHOLÆ REPANDUNENSI PROPE VIGINTI ANNOS PRÆPOSITI

UT INSIGNIA EJUS ERGA SCHOLAM ILLAM ANTIQUAM
BENEFICIA

MONUMENTO PERPETUO IN MEMORIAM REVOCARENTUR
HOC ÆDIFICIUM

AMICI ET DISCIPULI EJUS EXTRUENDUM CURAVERUNT.

A. S. MDCCCLXXXVI.

Portraits of Drs. Sleath, Peile, Pears, and Huckin, adorn its walls.

In 1888 the block of four Form rooms on the east side of the Priory was built, and a year later the old "Big School" was dismantled, its floor and ceiling were covered with oak, and, later on, its walls were panelled with oak, and shelves of the same material were affixed to them, it was fitted up with oak tables and seats, as a Sixth Form library. The inner room is about to be similarly fitted up. How former generations of O.R.s would stare if they could see the accommodation for the present Sixth Form ! When Dr. Bigsby was a boy at School " the chair and desk of the Headmaster were under the canopy of time-stained oak, on a raised stage or platform," at the north end of the room, " ascended, on either side, by steps The space thus separated from the floor beneath was formerly enclosed in the manner of a pew, and contained seats for the accommodation of nearly the whole of the Sixth or head form. The approach was by a door at either side, situate above the steps." This " pew," much to the sorrow of the Dr., was removed in the year 1821.

In 1883-4 the roof was raised, and new " studies " were built at the Hall. During the last ten years additional blocks of class rooms, laboratories, fives-courts, and a Porter's Lodge (the gift of the present Headmaster) have been added.

The last improvement is now (1899) being made. In the year 1890 the Governors acquired the freehold of the " Hall Orchard," at its south end a Sanatorium was erected and opened in the year 1894. The " Orchard," owing to the unevenness of its surface, could not be used, properly, for games, so subscriptions for levelling it were asked for, O.R.s and others responded, as usual, in a very liberal manner, and the work was commenced at the end of last year. When finished there will be three fine " pitches," one across the south end, and two, divided by a terrace, from it and themselves, down the remaining part of the " Orchard " Owing to the unevenness referred to it was impossible to make it of one level.

Mr   Estridge's   House.

Plate 14.

Mr   Gurney's   House.

CHAPTER XIII.

CHIEF EVENTS REFERRED TO, OR DESCRIBED.

A.D.

584-93   THE Kingdom of Mercia founded, Creoda its first King.

652   Peada, son of Penda, converted to Christianity, p. 8.

655-6   Penda, K. of Mercia, slain at Winwaedfield by Oswin, p. 8.

c. 656   Repton Abbey founded, p. 8.

657   Bishop Duima died, "buried among the Middle Angles at Feppingum" (Repton ?) p. 8.

660   Eadburgh, daughter of Aldulf, K. of East Angles, Abbess, p. 9.

672   Guthlac enters the Abbey, pp. 9—12.

c. 695   Ælfrida = (Ælfthryth), Abbess, pp. 9—12.

755   Æthebald, K. of Mercia, slain at Seccadune (Seckington, nr. Tamworth), buried at Repton, pp. 6—9.

781   Cyneheard, buried at Repton, p. 9.

835   Cynewaru, Abbess of Repton, p 9.

839   Wiglaf, K of Mercia, buried at Repton, p. 9.

849-50   Wystan, son of Wimund, murdered at Wistanstowe, Shropshire, by his cousin Berfert, the body was brought to Repton, and buried by the side of his grandfather Wiglaf, p. 15.

874   The Danes came to Repton, left again in 875, having destroyed Repton Monastery, &c., p. 9.

c. 957   Repton Church built, p. 9.

c. 1034 Canute transfers the relics of St. Wystan to
         Evesham Abbey, p. 9.

1086   Repton is mentioned in Domesday Book as
         having a church, two priests, and two mills,
         p. 9.

1172   The Canons of Calke transferred to Repton
         Priory, which had been built by Maud, Coun-
         tess of Chester, a few years before, c. 1150,
         p. 10.

1207   A portion of St. Wystan's relics returned to the
         Canons of Repton, p. 16.

1330   The owners of the Manor of Repton claimed to
         be lords of the hundred, and to have within
         their manor a pillory, tumbrell, and gallows,
         for the punishment of criminals; they also
         claimed, by prescription, a market at Repton
         on Wednesday, and a fair on the 1st of July.

1337-77 Repton Church enlarged to its present size, p. 20.

1538   Repton Priory dissolved, granted to Thomas
         Thacker in 1539, destroyed by his son Gilbert
         in 1553, p. 53.

1557   Sir John Porte founded Repton School, pp. 61—63.

1622   A Royal Charter granted by King James I.
         incorporating Etwall Hospital and Repton
         School, p. 64.

1643   The Inhabitants of Repton and other parishes
         protest against the marauding excursions of
         the Parliamentary forces, under Sir John
         Gell, quartered at Derby, p. 5.

1654   Thomas Whitehead, 1st Usher of Repton School,
         founded the Whitehead Charity.

1657   Ralph Hough Charity founded.

1687   The grave, with stone coffin, skeletons, &c.,
         discovered in Allen's close, p. 5.

1697   Mary Burdett Charity founded.

1699   The river Trent made navigable, up to Burton-
         on-Trent, by Act of Parliament.

1706   William Gilbert Charity founded.

1717   Dorothy Burdett's Charity founded.

1719   A singer's gallery erected at the west end of the Church, p 21.

1721   The Church spire rebuilt by John Platt and Ralph Tunnicliffe

1736   William Hunt's Charity founded.

1749   Richard Coming's Charity founded.

1766   The "Common" fields enclosed by Act of Parliament.

1779   The Crypt of Repton Church discovered ! p. 21

1784   The upper part of the Church spire, which had been struck by lightning, rebuilt by Mr Thompson of Lichfield

1792   The Church restored, p. 21.

1802   Repton volunteers enrolled (150.

1804   The weather-cock on the spire repaired by Joseph Barton

1805   Navigation on Trent ceased, transferred to Trent and Mersey Canal.

1806   The old square shaft of Repton Cross replaced by the present round one.

1815   The Methodist Chapel built.

1836   The Independent Chapel built

,,   Willington Bridge begun, opened in 1839

1838   The Church School-room built by public subscription.

1839   A two-edged sword, and a large quantity of human bones found, whilst digging out the foundations of the culvert bridge over the "Old Trent."

1842-8 Galleries on the north and south sides of the Church built, p. 22.

1843   A troop of yeomanry raised.

1851   The British Archæological Association visited Repton, from Derby

1854   The two round Saxon arches and piers removed, replaced by the two pointed arches, and hexagonal piers, p 22.

,,   Repton Institute opened.

1857   Repton School Tercentenary, p 75

M

1857   Repton Gas Company established.

1858   Repton School Chapel founded, p. 76.

1866   Tile Kiln discovered on the Paddock, p. 71.

1867   School Chapel enlarged by the addition of an apse, in memory of Mrs. Pears, p. 77.

1868   A new clock in the Church, also in her memory.

1874   Dr. Pears resigned, and Mr. Messiter died.

,,   Dr. Huckin, headmaster.

1880   School Chapel extended about twenty feet to the west, p. 77.

1883   Dr. Huckin died.   Rev. W. M. Furneaux succeeded.

1884-5 South Aisle added to School Chapel, p. 77.

1886   Pears School opened on Speech Day, June 17th, by the Hon. Mr. Justice Denman, (O.R.), p. 83.

,,   Repton Church restored, p. 23

1887   Engineering Works established by W. Stephenson Peach, Esq.

1888   The block of Form rooms erected on the east side of the Priory.

1889-91 Old " Big School " converted into " Sixth Form Library," p. 85.

1890   Freehold of Hall Orchard purchased, and Cricket Pavilion enlarged.

1891   Freehold of Hall and Cricket Field purchased.

1894   New Sanatorium opened.

1896   Porter's Lodge built.

1897   New Fives' Courts made.

1898   Willington Bridge made free for ever, on August 1st.

1899   Hall Orchard levelled.

Plate 15.

Cricket Pavilion, Pears Hall. &c.

CHAPTER XIV.

THE NEIGHBOURHOOD OF REPTON.

THE neighbourhood of Repton is full of objects of interest for the antiquary, geologist, botanist, or the lover of the picturesque.

Beginning with Repton, with its church, camp, &c., which date back to the 9th century, down to Stretton with its most beautiful 19th century church, the antiquary will find many objects of interest. The geologist will find much to interest him in the gypsum quarries and mines at Chellaston Hill, and the carboniferous limestone quarries at Tickenhall, Calke, and Breedon Hill. In the pages of " Contributions to the Flora of Derbyshire," by the Rev. W. H. Painter, the botanist will find a list of plants, &c., to be found in the neighbourhood. The lover of the picturesque will find much to please him in the varied scenery of the valley of the Trent, and its numerous tributaries. The views from such points as Askew Hill, Bretby Clump, King's Newton and Breedon Hill, are scarcely to be equalled in any county of England. The plan adopted in the following descriptions of towns, &c., is to group together those which lie close to one another, so that the visitor may visit them together in his walk or drive. All are within about eight miles of Repton.

ASHBY-DE-LA-ZOUCH.

What reader of " Ivanhoe " does not remember one scene, at least, in that well-known romance, " The Gentle and Joyous Passage of Arms of Ashby," which has shed such a lasting halo of chivalry over that town ? Sir Walter Scott had often stayed with Sir George Beaumont, at Coleorton Hall, and, no doubt, had visited all the places connected with the history of the locality. The Castle of Ashby in which " Prince John held high festival," as Sir Walter writes, " is not the same building of which the stately ruins still interest the traveller," but the description given of the field in which the tournament was held, corresponds, in a most minute manner, with the " Tournament Field," still so called, at the neighbouring village of Smisby, and has for ages been identified with that famous " Passage of Arms." Eight miles south-east of Repton this very interesting " habitation among the ash trees " is situated.

The first authentic mention we have of it is about the year 1066, when William the Conqueror granted the Manor to Hugh de Grentemaisnel, one of his most valiant captains at the battle of Hastings. In Domesday Book we read of its having a priest and church. Soon afterwards it fell into the hands of Robert de Beaumeis, another Norman, whose successor, Philip, granted " the church of St. Helen of Ashby, with the church of Blackfordby," &c., &c., to the Abbey of Lilleshall, Salop. Philip de Beaumeis, having no son to succeed him, left his estates to his daughter Adeliza, who married Alan la Zouche, a descendant of the Earls of Brittany. Alan settled at Ashby, and added the family name to it, to distinguish it from the other towns of that name. Alan was succeeded by his son Roger, who was succeeded by his son Alan, the last of the real Zouches, in the male line, who held the Manor of Ashby, he granted it to Sir William Mortimer, a distant relative, who assumed the name, and passed it on to his son Alan, who fought

Ashby Castle.

(Page 92.)

Plate 16.

Staunton Harold.

(Page 135.)

at the battle of Creçy, 1346, and died in that year, he was succeeded by his son Hugh, who died in 1399, leaving no heir, with him the name, finally, became extinct.

The property was held by Sir Hugh Burnett for about twenty years, when James Butler, Earl of Ormond (a Lancastrian noble), by some means or other, obtained possession of the land, he was executed at Newcastle after the battle of Towton Moor in 1461. In that year Edward, Duke of York, became King, and rewarded his partisans with titles and grants of land. Among them was Sir William Hastings, whom he created Baron Hastings of Ashby, &c., Steward of Leicester, and ambassador, with the Earl of Warwick, to treat for peace with Louis XI., King of France, who gave him a pension of 2000 crowns per annum. The first payment was made in gold, which Lord Hastings is said to have received with these words, " Put it here into my sleeve ; for other testimonial (receipt) you shall get none : no man shall say that King Edward's Lord Chamberlain hath been pensioner to the French King." This *may* be the origin of the crest of the Hastings' family, a maunch or sleeve. King Edward also gave him " licence to enclose and impark 3000 acres of land and wood at Ashby-de-la-Zouch," and to erect and fortify houses, &c., there and elsewhere. In the year 1474 he built Ashby Castle, nine years later the Protector (Richard, Duke of Gloucester) accused him of high treason, and, without trial, had him beheaded on a log of wood on Tower Green. His remains were interred in Windsor Castle, where a splendid monument was erected to his memory.

As we are not writing a history of the Hastings family, we must confine ourselves to those members of that family connected with the history of the place, which for two centuries centred round its castle and church. Ashby Castle was, as we have seen, built by the first Lord Hastings in 1474. It stands on the south side of the town. Judging by its ruins, it must have

been indeed a stately pile. Entering from the west we
see the remains of the kitchen, with its fire-places, &c.;
it had a groined roof, over which were rooms, with
another storey over them, access to these was obtained
by a spiral staircase in the north-east corner of the
kitchen. The west front of this block has been
destroyed, so nothing can be written about its chief
entrance, its height is about seventy feet, the dimensions
of the kitchen are fifty feet long, by twenty-seven broad,
and thirty-seven feet high.

In the kitchen are two doorways leading into the
" servants hall," from this two doorways lead into the
the Great Hall, and from this admission was obtained to
a " drawing room." At the end of this room, a little to
the south, is the chapel, lit by four windows, on either
side, and an east window. At the west end, over the
west door, is a gallery, to which a spiral staircase leads.
Adjoining the east end, to the south of it, were rooms
for the chaplain. On the south is a courtyard formed
by the chapel, chaplain's rooms, a thick wall, and the
Great Tower. This tower must have been an imposing
building of, at least, four storeys, with cellar, kitchen,
dining hall, drawing room, and sleeping apartments.
Its southern half is destroyed, but what is left on
the north side—turrets, windows, fire-place, armorial
bearings, &c., prove how richly the fabric was sculptured over. Very probably there was a wall from the
Great Tower on its west side, like that on its east side,
which met a wall built out from the kitchen. The
ground plan of the Castle would form a parallelogram
with kitchen, servants' hall, great hall, drawing room,
and chapel on the north side, chaplain's room at the
east end, Great Tower, with walls on the south side, and
a wall and kitchen at the west end. A subterraneous
passage connects the kitchen with the Great Tower.

The chief historical events connected with the Castle
are the visit of Mary, Queen of Scots, in November of
the year 1569. She was on her way from Tutbury to
Coventry. Anne, wife of James I., and Prince Henry

were entertained at the Castle in June, 1603, and King
James himself paid the Earl a visit in the year 1617.
The expenses of this visit were so great, the Earl's
income became seriously diminished, as one of his
descendants, Lady Flora, daughter of the 1st Marquis
of Hastings wrote, *a propos* of the visit,

> The bells did ring,
> The gracious King
> Enjoyed his visit much;
> And we've been poor
> Ere since that hour
> At Ashby-de-la-Zouch.

Again in May, 1645, another Stuart was a guest at
Ashby.   Charles I., flushed with the success of his army
at Leicester, spent a short time at the Castle.   Fifteen
days later, June 14th, he came again, this time a fugitive
from the fatal and final battle of Naseby Field.   The
Royalist garrison yielded Leicester, and marched out,
the Governor Hastings (Lord Loughborough) to Ashby,
the officers and men to Lichfield.   For months the
Parliamentary army, under Sir Thomas Fairfax, besieged
the town and castle, which held out bravely for the
Royal cause.   On the 28th February, 1646, articles of
agreement were drawn up, and signed by Lord Loughborough, and Colonel Needham.   The articles consisted
of eleven "items."   The officers and soldiers were
" to march away to Bridgenorth or Worcester, with
their horses, arms, and ammunition, bag, and baggage,
trumpets sounding, drums beating, colours flying," &c.,
or they might "lay down their arms, and have protection
to live at home if they please," " and the works and
fortifications of the town and garrison should be
sleighted," " after which the sequestrations of Colonel
General Hastings, the Earl of Huntingdon, should be
taken off," or " the Colonel General, with the said
gentlemen, could go to Hull or Bristol to have a ship
provided to transport them to France or Holland,
whither they please."   In 1648 the "sleighting" of the

Castle was performed, only too well, by one William Bainbrigg, of Lockington, in the county of Leicester. On the north side of the Castle was a green, on the south a garden, a wall, still existing, surrounded it with towers of brick, with stone facings, used as summer-houses, or "look outs." On the east of the Castle is a triangular tower, triangular in shape, called the "Mount House," it is said to be connected with the kitchen by a subterraneous passage. The "Manor House" on the north-east side, occupies the site of a suite of apartments made to accommodate King James I. in the year 1617.

Ashby Church, dedicated to St. Helen, occupies the site of an earlier building, probably Norman. During the fourteenth and fifteenth centuries it was rebuilt, and consisted of chancel, nave, north and south aisles, with tower at the west end. During the last twenty-three years nearly £16,000. have been spent in enlarging and restoring it. Now it consists of nave with two aisles on its north and south sides, all the galleries have been removed, and the old pews have been replaced by well-designed oak seats. The choir stalls are placed at the east end of the nave, leaving the chancel unoccupied. Over the altar there is a fine reredos of oak, ascribed to Grindley Gibbons. On the south side of the chancel is the mortuary chapel of the Huntingdon family. A most magnificent tomb of Francis, 2nd Earl of Huntingdon, and his wife Katherine, occupies the centre of it. Every detail of it is well worth a very close inspection. There are also many mural tablets in the chapel.

Within a sculptured recess in the north wall of the church is a finely executed figure of a pilgrim. Lying on his back, the head rests on a cushion, just above the right shoulder a portion of a pilgrim's hat with scallop-shell is seen. Round the shoulders, and over the breast, is the collar of SS. The figure is clothed with a long cloak, the feet, which rest on a dog, are shod with laced boots with pointed toes. Across the body is a pilgrim's staff, clasped by the left fore-arm, the hands meet over the breast, pressed together in the attitude of prayer, his scrip, ornamented with scallop-shells, is suspended, diagonally, from his right shoulder. The statue is supposed to be a Hastings, at least the family claim it, and have had their badge—the maunch—sculptured on the wall of the recess. Among other monuments in the church are those to Robert Mundy and his two wives, a very curious one to Mrs. Margery Wright with high-crowned hat, ruffles and ermine muff! and many modern ones. The most curious relic of mediæval days is an old finger pillory, formerly used for the punishment of disorderly-behaved persons in church. It is in front of the screen which separates the nave from the tower. The windows of the church are nearly all of stained glass, and illustrate scenes in the life of our Lord.

The town of Ashby is well known for its baths. In the year 1822 they were opened, but the great expectations of converting the town into a fashionable health resort have not been realized. The water is not found at Ashby, but is pumped from deep coal pits at Moira, some three miles distant, and conveyed to the baths in tanks specially constructed for that purpose.

Ashby received quite an unusual class of visitors in the year 1804. During the prolonged wars between England and France many thousands of prisoners were landed on our shores. According to Sir Archibald Alison there were no less than 50,000 French prisoners in Great Britain. For the accommodation of " the rank and file " such places as Dartmoor prison were erected, but the officers were quartered in different towns. On Friday, September 26th, 1804, the first detachment, consisting of forty-two officers, arrived in Ashby, other detachments followed, till about two hundred found lodgings there, among them were officers of the army and navy, and about thirty others described as merchants. They lived on excellent terms with the good people of Ashby for ten years, they were allowed liberty to walk a mile in any direction out of the town. Some escaped, and some were exchanged for English officers imprisoned in France.

N

Canon Denton, Vicar of Ashby-de-la-Zouch, has written a most interesting account of its castle, and this French occupation in " Bygone Leicestershire." He obtained the information about the latter, from the lips of one of his parishioners (Mrs. Whyman), who lived at the time, and saw them. He also had access to a diary kept by an Ashby physician (Dr. Kirkland). The church registers contain entries of marriages contracted between the officers and residents, also entries of baptisms and burials, which, as the Canon writes, " show, among other things, that the prisoners of war, who were quartered at Ashby, did not allow national prejudices to prevent them forming the closest ties with the inhabitants of the place of their captivity."

Little more remains to be written about this interesting town. Its Grammar School, founded in 1567 by the Earl of Huntingdon and others, augmented about thirty years after its foundation, by an inhabitant who is said to have lost his way, and was guided to his home by the sound of the church bell. In gratitude for this he conveyed to the trustees of the school certain property on condition that the bells " should be rung for a quarter of an hour at four o'clock in the morning." This custom was kept up till 1807, when it was discontinued. The property is still known as the " Day Bell Houses." One of the Headmasters was Dr. Samuel Shaw, son of Thomas Shaw, of Brook End, Repton, blacksmith, and was at Repton School under Dr. Ullock. At the age of 15 Samuel Shaw was admitted as a sizar at St. John's College, Cambridge. In 1658 he was Rector of Long Whatton, ejected in 1661, and was elected Headmaster of Ashby Grammar School in 1668.

On Thursday, July 24th, 1879, a memorial cross, in design like Queen Eleanor's cross at Northampton, was unveiled. It bears the following inscription, written by the late Earl of Beaconsfield : " In memory of Edith Maud Countess of Loudoun in her own right, Baroness Botreux, Hungerford, De Moleyns and Hastings, who sprung from an illustrious ancestry herself possessed

Barrow-on-Trent Church.

(Page 99.)

Plate 17.

Swarkeston House.

(Page 101.)

their noblest qualities, the people of Ashby-de-la-Zouch and the neighbourhood have raised this cross as a tribute of admiration and of love." The cross was designed by the late Sir Gilbert Scott, R.A., and executed by Messrs. Farmer and Brindley at a cost of £4,500.

BARROW, SWARKESTON, AND STANTON-BY-BRIDGE.

One of our pleasantest walks from Repton is to Barrow, down Brook End, up Monsel Lane, past the (Canons') Meadow Farm, and, by a field path to the left, to the river Trent, over which there is a ferry, to Twyford village. After passing through Twyford, turn to the right along the road, or by a field path, and the picturesque old village of Barrow will soon be reached. Barrow, most probably, derived its name from a barrow within the parish, which parish includes the villages of Arleston, Sinfin, Stenson and Twyford. Of these villages little can be written, Arleston has some ancient buildings and ruins which belonged to the preceptary of the Knights Templars or Hospitallers. Sinfin is noted only for its moor, on which the Derby races were formerly run. In the year 1804, it was enclosed by Act of Parliament, and divided among the adjoining townships.

Stenson and Twyford were manors belonging to the Ferrars at the time of the Domesday Survey, later on they passed to the Curzons, Findernes, and Harpurs.

The church at Twyford, dedicated to St. Andrew, is a chapelry of, and held by, the Vicars of Barrow. A Norman arch divides the nave from the chancel, the rest of the church is of the Decorated period. It has a tower terminated by an octagonal spire. There are three bells, and a few mural monuments to the Harpur, Vernon, and Bristowe families.

Barrow-on-Trent, as it is usually called, dates back to Norman days, when it had a priest and a church. One portion of the manor formed part of the endowment of the bishopric of Carlisle, the other, and proper manor, including the church, belonged to the ancient family of Bakepuz, one of whom, Robert de Bakepuz, gave the church to the Priory of St. John of Jerusalem, Knights Templars, or Hospitallers, who had a preceptory, as we have seen, at Arleston in the parish of Barrow. For a full and interesting account of the connection between Barrow and the Knights, see " Cox's Churches of Derbyshire," Vol. IV., pp. 11—19.

When the Order was dissolved in the reign of Henry VIII., the manor and advowson of the vicarage were granted to the family of Beaumont, and remained with them till 1638, since that time the advowson has very frequently changed hands, by sale, or otherwise. In 1638 Daniel Shelmerdine (an O.R.) was chosen and elected by the parishioners, and held the living till he was ejected in 1662. The church, dedicated to St. Wilfred, consists of nave, chancel, north and south aisles, south porch, and tower at the west end. There are now no remains of the Norman church. During the reign of Henry III. (1216—1272), the church was probably rebuilt, and again, in the Decorated and Perpendicular periods, alterations and additions were made. There are monuments in memory of the Bothes, Beaumonts, and Sales.

SWARKESTON.

At the time of the Domesday Survey, Swarkeston (Suerchestune or Sorchestun) was divided between the King and Henry de Ferrers. In the reign of Edward I. it belonged to John de Beke, or Beck, and Robert de Holland. Joan, wife of John de Beck, left it to her son and heir. In the fourteenth century the manor and

advowson was purchased by the Rollestons, of Rolleston,
in Staffordshire, with whom they remained till about the
middle of the sixteenth century when the manor passed
into the family of the Finderns. Jane Findern, daughter
and heiress of George Findern, conveyed it, by marriage,
to Richard Harpur, who built a mansion at Swarkeston.
This mansion was fortified, and the bridge defended by
earth-works, for the King, by Colonel Hastings in 1642.
In January, 1643, Sir John Gell marched against it with
Sir George Gresley's troops, the house was abandoned
on their approach, but the defenders of the bridge only
yielded after a stubborn defence.

Swarkeston Bridge is the most famous one in Derbyshire, and from end to end measures 1304 yards. The
modern part of the bridge, over the river Trent, is about
138 yards, the remainder forms a raised causeway, about
eleven or twelve feet wide, with arches, here and there,
so that the flood water can escape. The greater part of
the bridge is in the parish of Stanton-by-Bridge. There
is a legend that the old bridge was erected at the sole
cost of two maiden sisters, who lost their lovers when
attempting to ford the swollen waters, to pay a visit
to their betrothed ones. It is also said that the ladies
spent the whole of their fortunes on the bridge, and lived
a life of penury ever afterwards.

The earliest mention of the bridge, discovered by the
Rev. Charles Kerry, editor of the Derbyshire Archæological Journal, is in the *Hundred Rolls*, and is as follows :
" Inquisition held at Derby on the Feast of S. Hilary,
in the Church of S. James, anno 3 Edward I. (Oct. 1,
A.D. 1275). The jury reported that the merchants of
Melbourne passing over the bridge had for three years
withheld passage money and tolls, unjustly and without
warrant, to the prejudice of our lord the King and the
borough of Derby."

" The Patent Rolls give three pontages for Swarkeston ;
viz. :—2nd Pat., 18 Ed. II., m. 31. ; 1st Pat., 12 Ed. III.,
m. 26. This latter was granted to the men of Swarkeston
for four years ; the collectors of the bridge tolls being

Hugo de Calke, and John the son of Adam. Given at
Westminster, March 1st, 1338. The 3rd will be found
in 3rd Pat., 20 Ed. III., which refers to the ruinous state
of the bridge, and appoints John the son of Adam
de Melbourne, senior, and John the son of Adam de
Melbourne, junior, to receive tolls for the reparation of
the bridge for three years. Given at Reading the 28th
of December, 1347." A long list of things to pay toll,
and the amount varying from ¼d. to 6d. is given.

Another inquisition held at Newark, Oct. 26th, 1503,
refers to the chapel on Swarkeston bridge, and a parcel
of meadow land, lying between the bridge and Ingleby,
granted to the Priory of Repton for a priest to sing mass
in the Chapel, which had not been done for 20 years.

In 1745 "bonnie Prince Charlie," the Young Pre-
tender, marched from Derby, with his advanced guard, as
far as Swarkeston Bridge, but on the 6th of December
was compelled, most reluctantly, to commence a retreat
to Scotland, which ended in the fatal battle of Culloden
Moor.

The village, now chiefly known as a fishing resort,
with its church, and posting house, is pleasantly situated
on the banks of the Trent. The ancient church was
"restored" in 1876, that is to say, it was rebuilt, with
the exception of the tower and Harpur chapel. Beneath
an arch, to the north of the altar, is a raised tomb on
which is fixed a large alabaster slab, on this is carved
the effigies of a man and woman, the front of the tomb is
divided into four compartments, in the two middle ones
are figures of seven sons and seven daughters. Round
the margin of the slab is the following inscription :—

"John Rolston Esquire sũtyme lord of Swarkston
dysscysyd the iii. day of Decber ye yere of our lord
MCCCCLxxxij, and Susane hys wyffe dysscysyd the
23ᵈ of Decber the yere of our lord MCCCCLX and IV
on whose sowlys God have mcy."

On the south side of the chancel is the Harpur
mortuary chapel. In it are two large raised tombs, each
supporting a pair of recumbent effigies. One tomb is

that of " Richard Harpur one of the justyces of the
Comen Benche at Westminster and Jane the wife, sister
and heyre of and unto Thomas Fynderne of Fynderne
Esquyer. Cogita mori."

The other tomb bears beautifully-carved effigies of
Sir John Harpur and his first wife. Over the tomb,
on a tablet, is this inscription :—" In piam posteritatis
memoriam et spem certam futura· resurrectionis monu-
mentum hoc struxit Johannes Harpur Miles Filius
Richardi Harpur armigeri justiciarii de Banco Regio.
Cui uxorem ducenti Isabellam filiam Georgii Pierpont
militis, Deus amplam et fœlicem dedit filios filiasque
duodecium quorum nomina scutis infra præponuntur,
Mortem obiit sept° die Octobris Anno Domini 1627."
In front of the tomb, kneeling at a double prayer desk,
are the figures of seven sons, and five daughters.

STANTON-BY-BRIDGE.

Pleasantly situated on the high ground overlooking
the valley of the Trent is the village of Stanton-by-
Bridge (Swarkeston). The De Stantons were lords of
the manor for many generations. In the reign of
Edward III., John Frances of Tickenhall married
Margaret, daughter and heiress of John de Stanton, so
the manor passed to the Frances family, and remained
with them till an heiress of that house married Sir
Thomas Burdett, Bart., of Bramcote, Warwickshire.
About this time the manor was divided between the
Burdetts and Harpurs, each, in turn, appointing to the
living. Now it is in the sole patronage of the Harpur-
Crewe family.

The church, dedicated to St. Michael, is a small one,
about 60 feet long, and consists of nave, chancel, north
aisle, south porch with a bell turret on the west gable.
The chancel arch, a plain semi-circular one, is con-

sidered to be Saxon, and the south doorway, ornamented
with chevron, or zizag, and billet mouldings, is of the
Norman period, not later than Stephen's reign. There
are several remains of incised sepulchral slabs, and also
slabs of alabaster bearing incised effigies of the Sacheverell and Francis families. During a restoration in
1865, some of the older slabs were discovered, and were
placed as they are now.

About a mile south of Stanton is a farmhouse called
St. Bride's, supposed to be once a grange chapel of
Burton Abbey. Built into its walls are many remains
of Norman work, and in the yard are stone coffins, and
other fragments of worked stone.

BRETBY AND HARTSHORN.

Three miles south of Repton is the village of Bretby.
Like most of the land round, it used to belong to the
Earls of Chester, from them it passed into the hands of
the Segraves, who possessed, among other manors and
estates, Coton-in-the-Elms, Rosliston, Linton, and
Repton.

In 1300 John de Segrave received a license to castellate
his mansion at Bretby. Soon after it passed, with the
manor, into the families of the Mowbrays, Dukes of
Norfolk, and, through one of the co-heiresses of that
family, to the Berkeleys, who, in 1585, sold it to Sir
Thomas Stanhope, grandfather of Philip, 1st Earl of
Chesterfield, and now, by descent, it belongs to the Earl
of Carnarvon.

It is not known when the castle was pulled down,
but most probably in the days of Philip, 1st Earl of
Chesterfield (1585—1656), who built a mansion on the
present site, within the park. The old castle stood on
the land to the south-west of the church, the grass

Anchor Church.

(Page 123.)

Plate 18.

Bretby Hall.

(Page 104.)

covered mounds indicate the foundations of a very strong fortress, consisting of two courts.

The stones of the castle were probably used in the building of the mansion in the park, which must have been a grand place, built " in the midst of a large park, well wooded, and stored with several kinds of deer, and exotic beasts ; several fine avenues of trees leading to the house, which is of stone, *though not of modern architecture*, very regular, convenient, and noble, with a very curious chapel, (designed in the Grecian (Ionic) style, by Inigo Jones), very good outbuildings. The gardens, after the plan of Versailles, in the old grand style, with terraces, leaden images of wild beasts, fountains, labyrinths, groves, greenhouses, grottoes, aviaries, &c., &c.," the park, with its chain of fishponds, and fine timber, must have presented a scene of unsurpassed natural beauty. Amidst such surroundings, an open-air masque, written by Sir Aston Cokayne, was "presented at Bretbie in Derbyshire on Twelfth Night, 1639," before the Earl and Countess and a great company. The masque is printed in "Glover's History of Derbyshire," Vol. II., part I., p 184.

In November, 1642, during the Civil War, the house, which had been fortified by the Earl, witnessed another scene. Four hundred foot, with a party of dragoons and two sacres, under the command of Major Molanus, were sent to Bretby by Sir John Gell. They compelled the Earl, and his garrison of 40 musketeers and 60 horse, to abandon the house, and fly towards Lichfield. " Then the Countess was asked by the victorious officers to give 2s. 6d. to each soldier, to save the house from plunder, but she said she had not so much in the house ; they proposed 40 marks as a composition, to which she returned the same answer ; they then offered to advance it to her, but she declared she would not give them a penny ; then the soldiers plundered the house, but the officers saved her own chamber, with all her goods." (Sir John Gell's M.S. Narrative).

In the year 1780, the young Earl " was persuaded

o

'by an artful steward,' to pull down this splendid mansion and chapel, as being in a dangerous state of decay, though it was afterwards proved to have been very substantial." The gardens also suffered a like fate. Fortunately the fine cedar of Lebanon, planted in February, 1676-7, on the east side of the house, escaped destruction. It is considered to be the oldest in the kingdom, and still flourishes, braced together by iron chains, and is the chief object of admiration to visitors to Bretby and its park. The present house was begun by the 5th Earl, who died in 1815, when the building operations ceased. The architect was Sir Geoffrey Wyatville, assisted by Mr. Martin, the Earl's architect. A ground plan of the house is printed on page 187 of "Glover's History of Derbyshire," Vol. II., signed by W. Martin, architect and builder, September, 1828. When completed it will form a four-sided building, with a courtyard within it.

The church of Bretby, or rather the chapel, for it is one of the seven chapelries of Repton, was rebuilt in the year 1877, in the place of a very old building, built in the thirteenth century. It occupies the old site with the addition of an aisle, which forms a large pew for the noble owners, and a vestry, both on the north side. The village consists of a few scattered houses. To the east of the park is Bretby mill, on a small stream; which, rising in the Pistern hills, runs in a northerly direction, through Repton, till it joins the river Trent.

HARTSHORN.

About four miles south of Repton is the ancient village of Hartshorn, which at the time of the Domesday Survey belonged to Henry de Ferrers. Later on the Priory of Repton had lands, a moiety of a park, and the important right of free warren over the manor. According to the

list of patrons of the living, various families succeeded
to the manor, among whom are mentioned the de la
Wards, Meynells, Dethicks, the Earls of Shrewsbury,
and the Earls of Chesterfield. One of the rectors was
Stebbing-Shawe, jun.,(an O.R.,)editor of the *Topographer*,
and historian of Staffordshire. The church, which is
well placed on the higher part, with the rectory on the
east side of it, forms a very pleasing object from a
distance, a closer inspection reveals the fact that, at
the restoration of 1835, when the nave of the church
was rebuilt, cast iron windows, imitating Perpendicular
tracery, were inserted! The east window of the chancel,
of two lights, belongs to the Decorated period. The
embattled tower is a fair specimen of the Perpendicular
period, and contains a ring of five bells. Three of them
were placed there during the time of Stebbing-Shawe, sen.
The other two are of pre-Reformation date, and bear
well lettered inscriptions : " Hec Campana Beata
Trinitate Sancta Fiat," and " Ave Maria Gracia Plena
Dominus Tecum."

Under an arch in the north wall of the chancel is
an altar tomb, on which lie alabaster effigies of Hum-
phrey Dethick, and his wife Eliza, of Newhall. In
front of the tomb are representations of their six children,
three sons and three daughters. The father and one son
are clothed in plate armour. Above the tomb is a shield
bearing the quartered arms of Dethick, Allestree and
Meynell ; at the east and west ends are shields quartering Longford with Hathersaye, Deincourt and Solney ;
Dethick impaling Longford, and Meynell impaling
Longford.

Many other ancient monuments used to be in the
church, but they have been " made away with." There
is a fine old parish chest, seven feet long, in the vestry.

In Vol. VII. of the Derbyshire Archæological Society
there are many extracts from the parish records of Hartshorn : under the date 1612, an inventory of the church
goods is given, the first item mentioned is " a Comuio
Cupp of Silver wᵗʰ a plate of silver having Ihon Baptᵈ

head vppon it." This plate was photographed by Mr. Keene, of Derby, and a copy of it, with a descriptive note by Mr. St. John Hope, was published in Vol. VIII. of the Journal. From it we gather the following facts.

The "plate of silver" is a paten of silver-gilt, 5¼ inches in diameter. The rim is qnite plain, with the exception of four narrow lines engraved on the extreme edge. The centre has a circular depression, which again contains a slightly sunk sexfoil with the spandrils filled with a rayed leaf ornament. The central device is a Vernicle, (*i.e.*, the face of our Saviour, as transferred to the handkerchief of St. Veronica, and usually called a Vernicle). The churchwardens wrongly described it as the head of St. John the Baptist. Round the head is a nimbus, with rays issuing from it. There are three "hall marks," two of which, the maker's name, a Lombardic **ʢ** in a dotted circle, and a leopard's head crowned, are remaining; the third, the date letter, is obliterated, so it is impossible to say, with certainty, when it was made, but as this type of paten prevailed between 1450 and 1530, the opinion is that its date is about 1480.

The communion cup bears the London date mark for 1611-12, and the inscription :

Juſtus fide vivet + J + (R + C.
1612.

The letters **J. R. C.** probably stand for James Royll, Churchwarden, 1612, who, with Denis Hashard, made the inventory at that date.

EGGINTON, STRETTON, AND TUTBURY.

At the making of the Domesday Survey, the manor of Egginton was held by Geoffrey Alselin, and had a priest and a church. The Alselins' estates passed, through an heiress, into the family of Bardulfs. Under them the

Eggington Church

(Page 109).

Plate 19.

Willington Church.

manor was held by Ralph Fitz-Germund, whose son William Fitz-Ralph, Seneschall of Normandy, and founder of Dale-Abbey, gave it to William de Grendon, his nephew. In exchange for Stanley, near Dale-Abbey. William's wife gave it, as a marriage portion of her daughter, Margaret, to Robert Fitz-Walkelin, one of whose daughters married Sir John Chandos. At the death of his descendant, another Sir John Chandos, one moiety of the manor passed to his niece Elizabeth, daughter of Sir John Lawton, and wife of Sir Peter de la Pole, one of the Knights of the Shire in 1400, from whom it descended to the Chandos-Poles of Radbourne. Another daughter of Robert Walkelin, Ermentrude, married Sir William de Stafford, whose son, Robert, left it to five co-heiresses, and so their moiety became divided into many shares, which were re-united, by purchase, by the family of Lathbury. A co-heiress of Lathbury brought her moiety to Robert Leigh, of Whitfield, Cheshire. In the reign of James I., the estate passed to Anne, daughter of Sir Henry Leigh of Egginton, who married Simon Every, Esq., of Chard, Somersetshire, created 1st Baronet in 1641, ancestor of the present owner, a minor, the 11th Baronet.

As the manor of Egginton was divided into two moieties, so was the rectory. Dr. Charles Cox thus writes, " Early in the reign of Henry III., the two moieties of the rectory were respectively conveyed to the newly-founded abbey of Dale by Amalric de Gasci and Geoffrey de Musters." In consequence of this division there were two rectors. The abbots of Dale-Abbey continued to present till the year 1344, meanwhile the lords of the manor laid claim to it, and, from that time down to 1712, a series of law-suits were carried on, the result of which is that at the present time the patronage is in five parts; two turns belonging to the Everys, two to the Poles, and one to the Leighs. An account of the various claimants, &c., and a list of the rectors, will be found in Cox's Derbyshire Churches, Vol. IV. The church, dedicated to St. Wilfred, consists

of chancel, nave, aisles, and low west tower. At various
times the church has been added to, but it chiefly
belongs to the Decorated period, the tower is Perpendicular, as are some of the windows. In the south wall
of the south aisle are two recesses, one contains an
effigy of a lady, holding a heart in her hand, supposed to
be Elizabeth, co-heiress of Stafford, wife of William
Tymmore. On the walls, and floor of the chancel are
memorial stones, and monuments of the Everys, and
several rectors.

There are three bells, bearing the 'following inscriptions :

    I.   " I was recast again to sing
         By friends to country, church, and king.
         Thomas Hedderley, founder, Nottingham, 1778."

    II. " Ihc. Ave Maria gracia plena Dominus tecum."

    III. " I sweetly toling men do call
         To taste of meats that feeds the soole, 1615."
         Bell mark of Henry Oldfield.

The 2nd bell is supposed to be the only one left when
the others were sold for the repairing of Monks' Bridge.
The third bell is of the same date, and bears the same
inscription as the 2nd bell in Repton Church.

The old Egginton Hall, the seat of the Every family,
was destroyed by fire in the year 1736, and was rebuilt
by Sir Edward Every, Bart., from designs by Wyatt.
In the Hall there are five splendid pieces of tapestry,
made at Gobelin's, in Paris, by order of Sir Henry
Every, who died in 1709, before the order was completed. Four exhibit emblematic devices of the four
elements, earth, air, fire and water, and armorial bearings,
in each compartment.

Earth is represented by Ceres (Demeter) in her chariot
in a garden, with fountains in the background. By the
side of the chariot stands her daughter Persephone,
wearing a mural crown. Lions and other wild beasts
occupy the foreground, the bordering is composed of
fruit and flowers.

Air is represented by Jupiter and Juno throned on the clouds. Boreas blowing up a storm in the background, birds, storks, pelicans, &c., occupy the foreground.

Fire is represented by Vulcan working at his forge, attended by Venus and Cupid, at the back is a cave with a furnace in its recesses. Weapons, and instruments of metal form a bordering.

Water is represented by Neptune and Amphitrite, in a chariot drawn by sea-horses. The bordering is composed of seaweed, shells, coral, &c.

The fifth hanging has a representation of Venus, with a little Cupid standing before her, and has a pretty bordering of flowers, landscapes, and medallions bearing symbolical emblems, coats-of-arms, adorn the sides of the hanging. Le Brun, the famous director of paneling at the Gobelin's, is supposed to have designed the tapestry. For many years the hangings were locked up in "a great chest at Hodges's, the coachmaker, in Chandos Street," where they remained till 1750, thus escaping the fire of 1736, they were set up about the year 1760. In March, 1644, there was an engagement on Egginton Heath, between the Royalists and Parliamentarians, when both sides claimed the victory.

STRETTON.

Stretton is a little village about 3½ miles from Repton. Its name is derived from the Latin *strata*, a street, and as the old Roman Ickneild Street passes close to it no doubt that had something to do with its name. Within the last two years it has become noted to all who take an interest in churches, and works of art. Following the good example of his partners Bass and Ratcliff, and other successful brewers, John Gretton, now M.P. for South Derbyshire, has built a most beautiful church in his native village.

It consists of nave with aisles, central tower over the choir, and chancel. The east end of the south aisle is separated from it by an arch and a stone screen, with wrought iron gates, and forms a small chapel.

The east end of the north aisle is used as an organ chamber, with vestries for the clergy and choir behind it.

A cross, bearing an appropriate inscription, marks the site of the former church, a little to the south of the present one. No expense was spared in the construction of the church, and the greatest praise is due to the founder, architect, (Mr. J. T. Micklethwaite), builder, (Mr. Halliday of Stamford), and all concerned in the erection of one of the finest village churches in England.

Where everything is so well done, it may seem unnecessary to call attention to anything in particular, but the unusual beauty of design and material of the font, (Frostely marble,) surmounted by its ornate canopy of oak, the splendidly carved chancel screen, surmounted by a cross of exceptional size and beauty, (the work of Mr. J. E. Knox, of Kennington), the stone screen of the little south chapel, the reredos, of marble and alabaster, in the chancel, the oak seats in the nave, the choir stalls, the organ case and pulpit, the pavement of the choir and sanctuary, and the furniture generally call for more than a passing glance. In the chancel are three stained glass windows, symbolizing our Lord in His glory, &c., by Sir William Richmond. The tapestry in the chancel was designed by the late William Morris. The roof of the chancel is decorated with angels playing and singing " Gloria in excelsis," the nave roof is also painted from designs by Mr. Charles Powell, of London.

TUTBURY.

Sir Oswald Mosley, in his History of the Castle, Priory, and Town of Tutbury, suggests that the name is derived from Tuisco, a Saxon idol. At the Norman Conquest the town and castle were granted to Hugh de Abrincis, who held them for a time till he acquired the estates, &c., of the Earls of Chester, when the King conferred Tutbury on Henry de Ferrariis or Ferrers, who was one of the commissioners appointed to make the Domesday Survey. He rebuilt and extended the Castle, and founded the Priory.

His descendant, Robert de Ferrers, joined Leicester in a rebellion against King Henry III., which ended in Robert being fined £50,000. Unable to pay so large a sum, he forfeited his estates to the King, who granted them to his son Edmund, 1st Earl of Lancaster. Thomas, 2nd Earl of Lancaster, was attainted and beheaded after the battle at Boroughbridge, A.D. 1322. Tutbury Castle fell into a state of ruin, and remained so till John of Gaunt, 4th son of Edward III., rebuilt it. The only parts of this castle now remaining, are the gateway, and the apartments on the north side which were occupied by Mary, Queen of Scots, from January to December, 1585. Her son, James I., often visited the Castle, " not," as Sir Oswald writes, " to indulge melancholy reflections, but to gratify an occasional delight which he took in the diversion of hunting. His feelings were not much affected when he surveyed the late abode of his unfortunate mother, for extreme sensibility was not one of his foibles."

King Charles I. also paid several visits to it, and in 1642 the Castle was garrisoned for him, and placed under the command of Lord Loughborough. After many privations, the garrison, at last, yielded up the Castle on April 20th, 1646. By a vote on the 19th of July, 1647, the House of Commons ordered that "it should forthwith be rendered untenable." Its walls

P

enclose a space of about three acres. On the elevated mound, at its west side, the Julius Tower used to stand, now its site is occupied by an artificial ruin. A deep moat or foss surrounds three sides. Within the walls was a chapel, dedicated to St. Peter, the site of which cannot now be found.

The *Priory of Tutbury* was founded by Henry de Ferrers, A.D. 1080, and occupied the north side of the present church, which belonged to it. On the 14th of September, 1538, it was surrendered into the hands of King Henry VIII., when its revenue was valued at £242. 15s. 3d. All the Priory buildings were pulled down, with the exception of the magnificent Norman nave and west end doorway of the Priory church, which now form the present parish church.

The town is situated on the west bank of the river Dove, which used to drive several corn and cotton spinning mills.

To John of Gaunt, Tutbury owed two of its ancient institutions, viz.:—The Minstrel's Court and Bull Baiting. The Minstrel's Court was held every year on the day after the Assumption of the Blessed Virgin Mary, being the 16th of August, to elect a king of the minstrels, to try those who had been guilty of misdemeanours during the year, and grant licences for the coming year. Various, very curious customs were observed, which will be found in " The Book of Days," Vol. II., p. 224. The old horn, bearing the arms of John of Gaunt, impaled with Ferrers arms, on a girdle of black silk, adorned with buckles of silver, is now in the possession of the Bagshawes of Ford Hall, Chapel-en-le-Frith.

The Bull Baiting is supposed to have been introduced, in imitation of the Spanish bull-fights, by John of Gaunt, who assumed the title of King of Castile and Leon, in right of his wife. A bull was granted by the Prior of Tutbury, the poor beast's horns were sawn off, his ears and tail cut off, and his nose filled with pepper. Then the minstrels rushed after the maddened beast, and if they could cut off a portion of hair or skin before it

Etwall Church.

(Page 116.)

Plate 20.

Etwall Hospital.

(Page 119.)

crossed the river Dove, it belonged to the Minstrels, if it escaped it was returned to the Prior. The proceedings led to very great rows, and many returned home with broken heads, &c. In 1778 the Duke of Devonshire abolished the whole proceedings.

In 1831 some workmen, digging gravel out of the bed of the river, about thirty yards below the bridge, four or five feet below the surface of the gravel, discovered "upwards of 300,000 valuable coins," which Thomas, 2nd Earl of Lancaster, lost, together with his baggage, when he was attempting to cross the river, in flood. For five hundred years the coins, consisting of English, French, and Scottish pieces, had remained hidden below the bed of the river.

The chief attractions at Tutbury are the Castle, Church, and Glass-Works.

ETWALL AND ITS HOSPITAL.

Etwall is about four miles north-west from Repton, and six miles from Derby.

The manor belonged to Henry de Ferrers at the making of Domesday Survey, and included the lordships of Bearwardcote (its old moated farm-house remains), and Bumaston. Etwall was for a time in the possession of the Shirley family. In the year 1370 it was conveyed to the Abbey of Beauvale in Nottinghamshire. In 1540, King Henry VIII. granted the manor, together with the impropriate rectory, and the advowson of the vicarage, to Sir John Porte, Knight, one of the Justices of the King's Bench, father of Sir John, the founder of Repton School.

The church was granted by Roger de Pont l'Evêque, Archbishop of York, (1154—1181), to the Abbey of Beauvale or Welbeck, and belonged to it till it was granted to Sir John Porte, from whom, through his son Sir John, it passed to Elizabeth, his eldest daughter and

heiress, who married Sir Thomas Gerard, Bart., of
Bryn, County Lancaster, " who, on account of his
adherence to the Roman Catholic faith, and alleged
complicity in a plot for the release of Mary, Queen of
Scots, was imprisoned in the Tower of London, as a
recusant, during the years 1567—70, and again from
September, 1586, to August, 1588, when he was removed
for some months to an inferior jail, called the ' *Counter*,'
in Wood Street." Sir William Gerard, grandson of Sir
Thomas, sold the estate, and the advowson of the
vicarage, in 1641, to Sir Edward Moseley, who, five
years later, sold it to Sir Samuel Sleigh, whose co-
heiresses Margaret and Mary, by his second and third
wives, married James Chetham, and Rowland Cotton, of
Bellaport, Shropshire, the decendants of Rowland still
live at Etwall Hall.

The church, dedicated to St. Helen, consists of nave,
chancel, north aisle, south porch, and a low embattled
tower at its west end. Originally the nave was separated
from the north aisle by an arcade of four semicircular
Norman arches, supported by round piers with indented
capitals, the two arches, nearest the east end, have been
thrown into one, and a pointed arch substituted. The
chancel is Early English, but most of the church, including the tower, has been rebuilt in the Perpendicular
style. The chancel window of three stained glass lights,
representing the Crucifixion, is flanked by two small
square windows, a very unusual arrangement, they are
also filled with stained glass bearing the arms of the Sees
of Canterbury and Southwell. At the east end of the
north aisle is the Porte chapel, fitted up with carved
seats and a reading desk for the use of the " master and
poor men " of the Hospital. The seats used to be
between the belfry and north door, and the Porte chapel
partitioned off from the nave. Early in the century the
partition was taken down, and the seats removed to their
present position. Built on to the east end of the north
aisle is the Cokburne's memorial chapel, which blocks
up the east window of the Porte chapel. Two of the

Cokburnes were Vicars of Etwall, their chapel was built about the year 1830, it contains several mural tablets, and is now used as a vestry.

Since Dr. Cox wrote his account of the church, a much needed restoration has taken place. The galleries at the west end, and the plaster ceiling, have been removed, and new seats, of pitchpine, pulpit, prayer desk, &c., have taken the place of the old ones.

There are several monuments in memory of the Porte family. The oldest one is a brass in memory of Henry Porte, and Elizabeth his wife, and used to be on the floor of the chapel. It has been taken up, and used to block up a door on the north side of the chancel. Only the matrix of the brass of Henry is left, but his wife, clad in conventual dress adopted by widows, and his children, nine sons and eight daughters, remain. At the upper corners of the brass are two shields, one bearing a figure of our Lord, with the "orbs mundi" in His left hand, and the other the Blessed Virgin, and Child. Of the two shields at the bottom one bears the arms of Porte, the other has been taken away. Below, on a brass scroll, is an inscription :—

" Orate pro anabus Henrici Porte, et Elizabeth uxis ejus, qui quidem Henricus obiit in festo Sci Thomæ Marturis.

Anno Dni M. V. duodecimo quorum anabus propitietur Deus."

" Under the arche that is bytwene the chancell and the chapell, where I and my wyff had used commonly to knele," so did Sir John Porte, Justice of the King's Bench, by will dated January 19th, 1527, order that his body should be buried. Over the grave a monument was erected, on which rest the effigies of Sir John, and his two wives, Jane, daughter and heiress of John Fitz-herbert of Etwall, and Margaret, daughter of Sir Edward Trafford. The tomb has been much mutilated, the heads of Sir John and one of his wives have been knocked off. He wears his robes of office, with a collar and pendant. On the north side of the monument are shields bearing the arms of Porte impaling Fitzherbert, on the south Porte impaling the quartered coat of Trafford. The Porte motto, "Intende prospere," is frequently repeated on the cornice above, and the various emblems of the Passion are carved among the other decorations of the monument. Built against the south wall of the chancel is the "comely and handsome tomb of pure marble" of Sir John Porte, Knt., son of Justice Porte by his first wife Jane. "Set and fixed, graven in brass," are portraits of Sir John, his two wives, (Elizabeth, daughter of Sir Thomas Gifford, of Chillington, and Dorothy, daughter of Sir Anthony Fitzherbert), and his five children, two boys and three girls, all by his wife, Elizabeth.

Above the tomb, on a square slab, is a shield bearing the arms of Porte, surmounted by helmet and crest. On the tomb, at the top left-hand corner, a shield Porte, impaling quarterly of Gifford and Montgomery, in the right-hand corner Porte impaling quarterly of the two Fitzherbert coats. Below, set in three quatrefoils, are three shields, (1) Porte, (2) Porte impaling Gifford and Montgomery, (3) quarterly of four, Stanhope, Maloval, Longvillers, and Lexington impaling Porte and Montgomery.

Below the figure is the following inscription :—

"Under thys tombe lyeth buryed the Boodye of Syr Johu Porte Kingght sonne and heyre unto Syr Johu Porte one of the Justyces of ye Kyngs Benche at Westmynstr Elsebeth & Dorothe wyves to the same Sr Johu Porte the sonne whyche sonne dyed the syrt day of June Anno Dni 1557."

Etwall Hall came into lay hands after the dissolution of monasteries. It is a very plain building, built, or rather faced, with stone brought from the ruins of Tutbury Castle. Nothing worth seeing, but, for those who admire tapestry, there are two beautiful pieces. One representing a garden scene, with a pagoda-like

building, columns, flowers, fruit and Cupids. At the
bottom the goddess Diana and other figures. Another
piece represents scenes in the life of King David:
playing before Saul, Battle scene, Marriage with
Bathsheba. The border consists of a series of figures,
chiefly ladies, with dogs, fruit, and flowers.

ETWALL HOSPITAL.

Etwall Hospital was founded by Sir John Porte. By
Will, dated March 9th, 1556, he directed " that six of
the poorest of Etwall parish shall have weekly, for ever,
20d. apiece over and besides such lodgings as he or his
executors should provide for them in an almshouse, to be
built in or near the churchyard of Etwall, and that the
money so to be paid to the said poor should be had and
received out of the lands and tenements thereinafter
limited for the performance of his Will." These lands,
&c., were in Moseley, Abraham, and Brockhurst, in the
County of Lancaster. The Hospital was built as directed.
In 1622, (by letters patent, dated 20 June, 19 Jac. I.),
owing to the improvements of the lands, &c., and con-
sequent increase of funds, the number of poor men was
raised to twelve, and a Master of the Hospital was
appointed at a salary of £20. per annum. It was also
ordered that " every day twice the poor men should
repair to the church at Etwall, and there continue all
the time of divine service, and sermon, if any, except for
some just cause to be allowed by the master, and should
receive the sacrament three times every year at the
least ; . . . . . . and that every one of them
should have for their stipend or allowance for every
week 2s. 6d., to be paid to them monthly." The
original building having fallen into decay, the present
building was erected in the year 1681. Built on three
sides of a square, on the north side of Etwall churchyard, from which it is separated by iron rails and a low
wall, the Hospital consisted of twelve rooms and a lodge,

where the Master resided, (*i.e.*, a room in the north-west corner, (No. 5),) till 1812, when the "Master's Lodge" was built, about half of a mile away, on the road to Willington. A nurse used to live in the room, which has its entrance from the back yard, at the north-east corner, where there is a washhouse, &c., her duties were to nurse, cook, and wash for the almsmen who had no wives. This room is now occupied by an almsman, the nurse, if there is one, living elsewhere.

Over the door in the centre of the north side is the following inscription :

"Sr John Port, Knight, son of Sr John Port, one of the Justices of the Court of King's Bench, haueing by his last Will left an Estate for the Erection and Endowment of a Free Schole at Repton and an Hospital in this place, departed this Life June VI. MDLVII. the which Foundations hauveing been accordingly established, this Hospitall, through length of time falling to decay, was rebuilt, the Sallary's increased, the Alms Men augmented from VI. to XII. The Right Honourable Theophilus Earle of Huntingdon, the Right Honourable Philip Earle of Chesterfield, and Sr William Gerrard, Barronet, Heires Generall. to the Founder, being Governors, MDCLXXXI."

Over the inscription are three shields, containing the arms of the governors, quartering, or otherwise impaling, those of Sir John Porte, over these the shield of Sir John.

The almsmen used to wear blue cloth gowns, with a silver badge on the shoulder, bearing the arms of Sir John.

In 1825 the number of "poor men" was increased to sixteen, and the four rooms were added on the east side of the Hospital.

LIST OF MASTERS.

YEAR.
1622—1657 * Rev. John Jennings, M.A.
1657—1691 * Rev. John Jackson, M.A.

YEAR.

1692—1712 * Rev. Ellis Cunliffe, M.A., Jesus Coll., Cambridge, Fellow, B.A , 1671, M.A., 1675.

1713—1740 * Rev. James Cheetham, D.D.

1740—1746 * Rev. Henry Mainwaring, M.A., St. John's Coll., Cambridge, B.A., 1732, M.A., 1736.

1746—1785 * Rev. Samuel Burslem, M.A.

1785—1809 Rev. Joseph Turner, M.A.

1809—1821 Rev. William Beer, M.A.

1821—1832 Rev. John Chamberlayne, M.A., Formerly 2nd Master of Repton School.

1832—1842 Rev. William Boultbee Sleath, D.D., Formerly Headmaster of Repton School.

1842—1863 * Rev. William Eaton Mousley, M.A., Trinity College, Cambridge, B.A., 1839, M.A., 1842.

1863—1866 Rev. John Morewood Gresley, M.A.

1866   * Rev. David Crawford Cochrane, M.A., Trinity College, Dublin, B.A., 1857, M.A., 1860. Ox. Com. Caus. 1861.

FOREMARK AND ANCHOR CHURCH.

Foremark, or Fornewerke, as it was called in Domesday Book, when it belonged to Nigel de Stafford. After passing through the hands of various families, it finally belonged to the Verdons, through the Verdons to Sir Robert Francis, who purchased it from them. The heiress of Sir Robert Francis married Thomas Burdett, Esq., of Bramcote, created a baronet in 1618, and it still belongs to that family. It and Ingleby are mentioned as Chapels of Repton as early as the thirteenth century. In 1650 a report was made by Parliamentary Commissioners, from which we gather that Ingleby was to be disused, and Foremark made the parish church. Owing

* Also Vicars of Etwall.

to the ruinous state of both chapels, Foremark was rebuilt, and Ingleby was demolished, its wood and stone
were used to build the bell-tower and churchyard wall of
Foremark. On the Feast of St. Matthew, 1662, the new
chapel was consecrated by Bishop Hacket.

The position of Ingleby Church, and the reason why it
was not restored, have been clearly pointed out, in a letter,
to Dr. Cox, by Mr. C. S. Greaves, Q.C., "the chapel of
Ingleby stood at the corner of a field, bounded by the
road through the village on one side, and by a wall of a
farm-yard on the other, occupied in my time by Browne.
It was the nearest farmyard to Derby. The course of the
walls was plainly indicated by the raised ground where
they had stood. When the present church (of Foremark)
was in contemplation, the then Baronet (Sir Robert
Burdett) told the inhabitants that if they would draw the
stone for the church, he would build it wherever they
liked; but if they would not, he would build it where he
liked. They refused, and accordingly it was built where
it was most convenient for the Hall, and most in-
convenient for Ingleby." See Addenda, Derbyshire
Churches, Vol. IV., p. 530.

Dedicated to St. Saviour, the chapel consists of nave,
chancel, and west tower, in the later Perpendicular style.
The chancel is separated from the nave by a high oak
screen, glazed with large sheets of glass. The altar, a
large slab of grey marble, supported by a wooden table,
is, according to Dr. Charles Cox (from whose "Notes
on the Churches of Derbyshire" these particulars have
been taken), the one consecrated by Bishop Hacket.
There are four five-light windows in the east end, and
sides of the chapel. A gallery was erected in 1819.

In the bell-tower are four bells bearing the bell-mark
of George Oldfield with the following inscriptions: —

    I. "Let God arise and his enemies bee scattered.
       1668."
    II. "Saint Savior. 1668"
    III. "All glory bee to God on high. Saint Saviours."
    IV. "God save his Church. 1660."

To the east of the church is Foremark Hall, it occupies the site of the old hall, " the seat of the Francis family, it was a long, low, half-timbered structure, with a garden occupying about two acres, in the centre of which was a large dove-cote."

In the year 1755 the present Hall was built. To the south-west of the Hall, in a secluded dell, is a ruined house called "Knowl Hills." Bigsby says it was erected by Walter Burdett, younger son of Sir Robert Burdett, Bart., the first possessor of Foremark. Until the erection of the Hall it was occupied by another Sir Robert Burdett, Bart. Then a greater portion of this singularly beautiful retreat was destroyed, but a grove of beech and lime trees still afford a grateful shade on a lawn where, during the summer months, " parties " are, or used to be held. There are also some very curious cellars excavated in the red sandstone rock beneath.

ANCHOR CHURCH.

About two miles to the east of Repton the level meadow-land of the Trent valley suddenly rises and forms a perpendicular bank, composed of conglomerate rock, with bands of sandstone. The Trent, which used to flow close to the bank, now flows at some distance away, the old course is still indicated by a pool of sedge-girdled water, (close in front of the rock,) which joins the river a little lower down. The face of the rock is irregular and broken into picturesque bays, with ivy-covered fissures between them, the whole crowned with trees, brushwood, and bracken.

Here, ages ago, an Anchorite is supposed to have scooped out of the rock an oratory and a dwelling, similar to that in Deepdale, (Dale Abbey). Here he dwelt, far from the haunts of men, in quietness and solitude. Who he was? who made it? and when? are questions that can never be answered, the only reference to it is found in the Repton Church Register under the year 1658. " Ye foole at Anchor Church bur Aprill 19." In later days it became the favourite retreat of Sir Robert Burdett, who had it fitted up so that he and his friends could dine within its cool, and romantic cells. It has been enlarged at various times, at present it consists of a series of four cells. Admittance is gained through an arched door-way, the first cell has been divided into two by a brick wall, plastered over, a small one on the right hand (10 ft 6 in. by 6 ft. 6 in.) with a small window, and a larger one (13 ft. by 12 ft. 6 in.) with a window in front, and two semicircular recesses at the back ; between this and the next cell two arch-ways have been made through the rock, with a pillar between them, also of rock, this cell is 17 ft. 6 in. by 13 ft. 6 in., and also has two similar recesses ; through another arch the last cell is reached (18 ft. by 17 ft.), this has three recesses, and two windows. The ground plan is semicircular, so that the last cell projects some distance out, and affords most extensive views of the valley of the Trent, and the country to the north and west, including Twyford and Repton. A little distance to the west is another cell (6 ft. by 4 ft.) commonly known as the Anchorite's " larder."

The best way to get to the " Church " is, after passing in front of Foremark Hall, and through a gate which blocks the road, to mount the hill, and enter a field through the first gate on the left hand, cross the field diagonally till a grassy glade is reached, which leads down to a wicket gate on the right, the entrance to the " Church."

MELBOURNE AND BREEDON.

Melbourne was in very ancient times a royal manor, and is mentioned in the Domesday Survey as having a priest and a church. It remained in royal hands,

Brecdon Church.

(Page 125.)

Plate 21.

Melbourne Church.

(Page 125.)

attached to the Earldom and Duchy of Lancaster, till
the year 1604, when King James I. granted it to
Charles, Earl of Nottingham, who conveyed it to Henry,
Earl of Huntingdon, from whom it descended to Francis,
Marquis of Hastings, now represented by the Earl of
Loudoun.   There used to be a castle here, in which
John, Duke of Bourdon, was imprisoned for 19 years,
after his capture at the battle of Agincourt, in 1415.
Queen Margaret, wife of Henry VI., is said to have
ordered it to be dismantled in 1460, and it gradually fell
into decay, only a few traces of it can now be seen.

The name Melbourne is derived from Mael-burn, two
Anglo-Saxon words meaning the " brook of the Cross."
A tradition exists that a cross was erected by the side
of the brook, which runs on the south side of the town,
to commemorate the murder of Osthryth, Queen of
Ethelred, King of Mercia (675—704).   Later on a small
church was erected over the spot, which was replaced by
the present one, " one of the finest and most interesting
Norman churches in England—and the earliest date we
are inclined to assign to its commencement is *circa* 1090."
Originally the church consisted of nave with side aisles,
central tower, with north and south transepts, three
apses at the east, two western towers, with a recessed
doorway between them.   Galleries, supported by groined
stone roof over the western portico, extended over both
aisles and central tower, two spiral stone stairs in the
western towers led up to the galleries.   Five " horse-
shoe " arches, ornamented with chevron or zigag mouldings, resting on round pillars, 4 ft. in diameter, and
15 ft. high, separate the nave from the aisles, the capitals
are square, with slightly indented mouldings.   The
triforium on the north side has triple round arches, that
on the south, of later date, has double pointed arches.
The central tower, on the inner sides, is divided into
three tiers of semi-circular arches.   The three apses at
the east end were removed probably during the reign of
Henry VII.   A square end was then made, and is lit by
a five-light Perpendicular window.   The apse arches

in the transepts were built up and a three-light
Decorated window was placed in the south, and a three-
light Perpendicular window was placed in the north
transept. Later alterations and additions have been
made which certainly have not added to the beauty of
the church, but, in spite of these, the church remains,
as Dr. Cox writes, " one of the finest and most interesting Norman churches in England," and well worth a
visit.

In the year 1132 Henry I. founded the bishopric of
Carlisle, and granted the church to it as one of its
endowments. The bishops built a palace at the east
end of the church, where they lived occasionally.
Melbourne Hall, built on the site of the palace by
Sir Thomas Coke, Chamberlain to Queen Anne,
possesses one of the most beautiful gardens in the
kingdom, laid out in the old Dutch style, it affords a
favourite place of resort to many who visit its sylvan
retreats during the summer months. They are open to
the public on Wednesday afternoons.

About a mile from Melbourne is the village of *King's
Newton* with its picturesque ruin, the remains of an
Elizabethan Hall, the ancient residence of the Hardinge
family. About thirty-five years ago it was burnt down.
King Charles I. is said to have been entertained here by
Sir Robert Hardinge. After the King's departure, some
lines were discovered written on a pane of glass, and
signed " Carlos, Newton Regis," which accounts for the
name. The view from the terrace is a very extensive
one, over the valley of the Trent, with Derby and the
high lands of the Peak district in the distance.

Breedon village is about two miles and a quarter from
Melbourne, it lies at the foot of a singular looking hill
which rises suddenly out of the plain. While all round
is marl and sandstone, this hill is composed of mountain
lime-stone. Rising to a height of about one hundred
and fifty feet, it is seen for miles round, and is known as
"*the Bulwark*," and was once an ancient camp. Its
sides have been quarried, and lime kilns at its base, when

at work, do not improve the air. On its summit is a
church, all that remains of a Priory of Austin Canons,
built in Norman times. There is a legend which
accounts for its exposed position. It is said that evil
spirits interfered with its erection at the foot of the hill,
and removed the foundations as often as they were laid.
In vain were exorcising prayers offered up, what was
done in the day was removed at night, so the materials
were carried up to the top, and the church was allowed
to be built, in it have been laid to rest members
of the Ferrers, Curzons, and Shakespear families. The
Ferrers' pew, separated from the church by iron bars,
surmounted by large escutcheons, is a rare example of
the luxury, selfishness, and exclusiveness which animated
the feelings of " the quality " in bygone times.

MICKLE-OVER, FINDERNE AND POTLAC OR POTLOCK.

The manor *Mickle-Over* with the three chapelries of
Finderne, Little-Over, and Potlac, was granted by William
the Conqueror to Burton Abbey, and it remained with it till
the dissolution of Monasteries, when Henry VIII. granted
the manor to his secretary, Sir William Paget. Thomas,
Lord Paget, sold the manor to the famous Lord Mayor
of London, Sir Thomas Gresham, whose widow married
again, and left the property to Sir William Reade, her
son by her second husband. Sir William Reade's
daughter and heiress married Sir Michael Stanhope, and
had three daughters, co-heiresses, between whom the
estates were divided. In 1648, Edward Wilmot bought
two shares, *viz.*, Little-Over and Finderne, which were
again sold by Sir Robert Wilmot to Edward Sacheverell
Pole in 1801. The remaining share, Mickle-Over, was
sold to Sir John Curzon in 1648, from the Curzons Mr.
Newton bought it in 1789. An ancestor of Mr. Newton
who died in 1619, had previously inherited the manor-

house of Mickle-Over by marriage with the heiress of
William Gilbert, to whom it had been sold by Sir
Thomas Gresham. The house is now occupied by the
tenant of the farm.

Little-Over is about two miles from Mickle-Over, and
used to be the seat of the Harpur family, Chief Justice
Sir Richard Harpur built the manor-house, in which the
family lived till the days of John Harpur, who died in
1754, when the property passed to the Heathcotes. In
the church is a costly monument to Sir Richard Harpur,
son of the Chief Justice, and his wife Mary, daughter of
Thomas Reresby. The church consists of nave, chancel,
north aisles, and bell turret on the west gable. The
blocked-up Norman doorway in the west end is the only
relic of ancient days.

Finderne is a small village, about two miles from
Repton. It had a very interesting old chapel, dating
back to its Norman days, but in the year 1862 it was
completely destroyed. It must have been like the chapel
at Little-Over. The present church consists of nave,
chancel, and tower, with a spire at the west end. The
only relic of the Norman church are the tympanum of
the old south door, carved in chequered pattern, with a
cross *formée* in the centre, and a recessed founder's
arch in the north wall of the chancel, which contains a
much mutilated effigy of a priest.

The most valued possession of the church is a small
chalice and cover, considered to be the oldest piece of
church plate in the county. The Hall-mark shows it to
be of the year 1564-5.

The Vicar of Finderne, the Rev. B. W. Spilsbury,
has in his possession a very curious and rare relic of
mediæval times. It is a small sculptured block of
alabaster, 8¾ inches by 7 inches, and 1½ inches thick.
There is a beautifully drawn and painted copy of it in
Vol. VIII. of the Derbyshire Archæological Journal,
by Mr. George Bailey, also an article on it by the
Rev. J. Charles Cox.

A little above the centre, resting on a dish, is a head,

below it is a lamb lying on a missal or book. On the right side is a bare-headed, full length figure of St. Peter, holding a key in his right hand, and a book in his left. On the left side is a similar figure of an archbishop, with a mitre on his head, a book in his right hand, and a cross-staff in his left. The back ground, *i e* the surface of the block, is painted a dark olive green. The head, dish and robes an orange brown. The hair, rim of the dish, and edges of the robes, books, key, and cross-staff are gilded. The lining of St. Peter's robe is red, that of the archbishop is blue. The head and dish occupy three quarters of the space. Dr. Cox enumerates ten similar pieces of sculpture, all of which have figures of St. Peter on the right side, and all, except one which bears a figure of St. Paul, have a mitred archbishop on the left, which is supposed to represent either St. Augustine, or St. Thomas of Canterbury. The chief differences are in the figures above and below the central head and dish. There is a cut on the forehead over the left eye. Several suggestions have been made respecting the head. It has been said to represent (1) The head of St. John the Baptist, (2) The Vernicle, (3) The image of our Lord's face, given to King Abgarus, and (4) The First Person of the Holy Trinity. Which of these is right is a matter for discussion, but "the block, no doubt, has reference to the presence of our Lord in the Sacrament."

At the back there are two holes, into which pegs could be inserted, for the purpose or fixing it above an altar, on a reredos or otherwise, in oratories or chantries. All the examples known were made about the same date, at the end of the fourteenth or the beginning of the fifteenth century.

The Vicar of Finderne also has an old deed, dated 1574, which sets forth that, in that year, Sir Thomas Gresham sold his property at Finderne, with manorial rights, to twelve men whose names are given. He had 1272 acres in Finderne, and 378 at Potlock.

Potlac or Potlock was the seat of the old family of Finderns, who for nine generations lived here (as tenants

R

under the Abbots of Burton), from the reign of Edward
III. to Elizabeth, when Thomas Finderne died, in
1558, leaving all his estates, here and elsewhere, to his
sister Jane, who married Sir Richard Harpur, one of the
Justices of the Common Pleas, ancestor of Sir Vauncey
Harpur-Crewe, Bart., of Calke Abbey.

The ancient manor house, and chapel, dedicated to
St. Leonard, have disappeared. A farmhouse occupies
the site of the former, and only a few cedar trees and
Scotch firs remain near the house to connect it with
the past.

NEWTON SOLNEY.

About a mile and a half from Repton, situated on the
banks of the Trent, is the pretty village of Newton
Solney. To distinguish it from the hundred or more
Newtons, the name of the ancient owners Solney or
Sulney is joined to it. The manor was held, in the
reign of Henry III. (1216-72), by Sir Norman, who was
succeeded in turn by Sir Alured, Sir William, and
another Sir Alured de Solney, who came to the rescue
of Bishop Stretton at Repton in 1364 (*see p.* 52). Sir
Alured died at the beginning of the reign of Richard III.
(1377-99), and left a son Sir John, who died without
issue, and two daughters, Margery, who married Sir
Nicholas Longford, and Alice, married three times,
(1) Sir Robert Pipe, (2) Sir Thomas Stafford, (3) Sir
William Spernore. During the reign of Henry VIII.,
the manor was bought of the Longfords by the Leighs.
Anne, heiress of Sir Henry Leigh, married Sir Simon
Every in the reign of James I.

Abraham Hoskins, Esq., purchased the estates from
Sir Henry Every, Bart., about the year 1795, and took
up his abode there. In the year 1801 he erected a

range of castellated walls, called "Hoskins Folly," on the high land between Newton and Burton, as a kind of look-out over the surrounding country, later on, he converted it into a house and called it "Bladon Castle." Mr. Robert Ratcliff is now the owner of the manor and patron of the living, which is a donative. Besides "Bladon Castle" there are two principal houses, one occupied by Mr. Ratcliff called Newton Park, and the "The Rock" occupied by Mr. Edward D. Salt.

The picturesque church, which has been carefully restored, contains specimens of all the styles of architecture from the Norman, downwards. It consists of nave, chancel, north and south aisles, with chapels, at the east end, separated from them and the chancel by pointed arches. The chancel arch was probably removed during the Perpendicular period.

There are three very ancient monuments of knights, which are well worth a close inspection.

The oldest of them is now lying under an arch at the west end of the south aisle, it is the freestone effigy of a mail-clad knight, with a shield on his left arm, his hands are on a sword, suspended in front on a cross-belt, unfortunately the effigy is much mutilated, the lower part has gone.

The second, also of freestone, is under the tower, on the north side, the head has gone, the figure is clad in a surcoat, girded by a sword belt, parts of armour are seen in the hauberk, the feet rest on foliated brackets of Early English work.

The third, on the south side, opposite number two, is a very beautiful effigy in alabaster, resting on an altar tomb of the same material. On the sides are eleven shields. The effigy will well repay a very close inspection, it is one of the most highly finished in the county. From its head (wearing a bassinet) down to its feet, every detail has been elaborately worked out. Most probably the monuments represent three members of the de Solney family, but which is a matter of discussion.

The effigy of Sir Henry Every, Bart., has been transferred from the chancel and placed beneath the west window of the tower. It is of marble, and the effigy is clad in a toga and sandals of a Roman citizen, the contrast, between it and the other two ancient ones, is most striking! On the front of the monument is the following inscription :—

"Here lies the body of Sr Henry Every, late of Egginton in this county, Baronet, who died ye 1st day of Septr 1709. To whose memory Ann his beloved wife, the eldest daughter and one of the coheiresses of Sr Francis Russell, late of Strentham, Bart. (of a very ancient family in ye county of Worcester) erected ye monument."

The floor of the tower has been paved with encaustic tiles found during the restoration, they are supposed to have been made at Repton.

Since Dr. Cox wrote his article on Newton Solney Church the restoration, referred to above, has been made, the whole of the fabric has been very carefully restored, a new south porch, of stone, has taken the place of the former brick one, the floor has been lowered and paved with stone, with blocks of wood under the pews, which are also new, of pitch pine.

TICKENHALL, CALKE, AND STAUNTON HAROLD.

About four miles to the south-east of Repton is the village of Tickenhall, which was formerly one of the seven chapels of Repton. At the time of the Domesday Survey its lands were divided between the King, Nigel de Stafford, ancestor of the Gresleys, and the abbot of Burton. Subsequently King Henry I. granted it, with Repton, to Ralph, Earl of Chester. From charters, quoted in Vol. II. of the *Topographer*, we learn that the

Canons of Repton Priory obtained grants of land and permission to draw a cart load of wood daily from the woods in Tickenhall, also the right of free warren over the land and fishing in the river Trent, from later Earls of Chester, and others. From the same source we learn that the chapel was originally dedicated to St. Thomas à Becket.

After the dissolution of monasteries, the rectorial tithes passed to Edward Abell, lord of manor of Tickenhall, who died in 1596. From his son, Ralph, Sir John Harpur purchased the manor and impropriate tithes in 1625, and they remain in the hands of his descendant, Sir Vauncey Harpur-Crewe, Bart., who is also the patron of the living, which has been converted into a vicarage in modern times.

In the year 1841 it was decided, at a vestry meeting, to build a new church, the old one being so much out of repair. About fifty yards to the north of the old one the present church was erected, consisting of nave, with aisles, chancel, vestry, and tower with spire. The picturesque, ivy-clad remains of the old church in the churchyard, the four-clustered pillars in the vicarage garden, and other fragments found *in situ* prove that the old Chapel of St. Thomas contained portions of Norman, Early English and Decorated work, and the fact that gunpowder had to be used in its demolition also proves that a most interesting church, connected with centuries of the history of Tickenhall, was destroyed. As if to complete the severance, the name of its patron saint was also changed to that of St. George, not in honour of England's patron saint, but after Sir George Crewe, Bart., lord of the manor, and patron of the living !

Formerly a good trade was carried on in the limestone quarries, but of late they have been closed. The " caverns " present a most picturesque appearance, and afford a grand field for the geologist in search of fossils, which abound in the carboniferous limestone there. There was also a pottery works, with a kiln, which have also been closed and pulled down. There is a hospital, founded by Mr. Charles Harpur in the year 1770, for " decayed poor men and women in the parishes of Tickenhall and Calke." It is now only occupied by women. The octagonal brick-built " round house " still remains by the side of the main street, and forms a link between the old and the new.

Calke was, as we have seen, celebrated for its " Abbey," the mother of Repton Priory. In the year 1547 Calke was granted by Edward VI. to John, Earl of Warwick. Thirty years later it became the property and seat of Roger Wendesley, whose successor, Richard Wendesley, sold it to Robert Bainbrigge, who in 1621 conveyed it to Henry Harpur, who was made a baronet in 1626. At the beginning of the eighteenth century the present " Abbey" was built on the site of the old priory, as it ought to have been called.

The parish church belonged to the Canons of Calke from the earliest times, and with them was transferred to Repton Priory, with whose canons it remained till the dissolution of the monasteries, when it passed to the owners of the estate

The Parliamentary Commissioners in 1650 describe Calke " as a peculiar Sir John Harper of the same Baronett is impropriator and procures the cure supplied. It lyes neare unto Ticknall and may conveniently be united to Tycknall and the chapell of Calke disused." There is a seal of the peculiar, a diamond in shape, with the side view of a man in a long gown. These words are round the margin, *Sigillum officii pecularis jurisdictionis de Calke.* As " peculiars " are exempt from the jurisdiction of the Ordinary or Bishops Courts, no doubt this seal was used for stamping deeds, &c., issued by the peculiar.

The church is said to be dedicated to St. Giles, who was also the patron saint of the priory. Sir George Crewe rebuilt, or rather re-cased, the old church with new stone in the year 1826. Like the windows at Hartshorn, the mullions and tracery are of cast iron, by Weatherhead, Glover and Co., Derby.   At the west end is a small embattled tower, in which is a door, the only entry to the church.

The village consists only of a few houses, but it is very prettily situated.

A little to the south-east of Calke is *Staunton Harold*, the seat of Earl Ferrers.   At the time of the Domesday Book Survey, the Ferrers family possessed estates in fourteen counties, and no less than one hundred and fourteen manors in Derbyshire.   Their principal seat was at Tutbury Castle in Staffordshire, where they founded the priory.   Robert, the 2nd Earl, was created Earl of Derby in the year 1138.   This title remained in the family till the reign of Henry III., when another Robert (the 5th Earl) was deprived of his titles and estates owing to his repeated acts of rebellion.   According to Lysons, the title was conferred on several Plantagenets. Henry VII. conferred it, after the victory of Bosworth Field, in consideration of services received, on Lord Stanley, in whose family it still remains.   The present Earl Ferrers is descended from Sir Henry Shirley, who married Dorothy, co-heir of Robert Devereux, Earl of Essex, and of the Baronies of Ferrers of Chartley and Bourchier.   Their grandson Robert was summoned to Parliament, by Writ 14th December, 1677, as Baron Ferrers of Chartley, and was created Viscount Tamworth and Earl Ferrers 3rd September, 1711.   Staunton Harold Hall was built by the 5th Earl Ferrers.   Situated in a lovely valley, overlooking a lake, bounded by sloping ground adorned with trees, and other shrubs, the house is one of the finest of its kind among our "stately homes of England."   It is built in the style of Andrea Palladio (Classical or Renaissance) with a pediment supported by Ionic pillars, which are upheld with Doric columns. The material is stone, or brick ornamented with stone. The south-west front, built in the form of the letter H, is surmounted with the statue of a huge lion.   The north-east, or library front, was designed by Inigo Jones.   The entrance gate of the Hall is of most elaborate and

beautiful specimen of iron workmanship. By the side of
the lake is a beautiful little Gothic church, consisting of
chancel, nave and two aisles. The chancel is separated
from the nave by elegantly wrought iron gates, which
bear the Ferrers' arms. From the walls of the church
are hung funeral trophies of the family, like those in
St. George's Chapel, Windsor.

Plate 22.

Tickenhall Round House.

(Page 134.)

INDEX.

S

THE END.